The Good,
The Bad and
The Pirate

by Mike Riley

Hand Published and printed aboard the ketch Beau Soleil

By, well, Me

on recycled paper

ISBN 978-0-9828247-2-6

sailingbooks@rocketmail.com

Dedication

I have always wanted to dedicate a book to a beautiful woman. It has been a life long dream. This is my chance. But I am going to double dedicate it to two women, to double my pleasure as they say.

To my Mother, Joann Riley, an icon to the belief that fun starts at home as does personality. Thanks, Mom, for an interesting childhood. It was great!

To my wife, Karen Riley, a person who has more good in her soul than all the rest of the world put together, thanks for rescuing me from my wild past.

Thanks, girls. Thanks, ever so very much.

Author's Note

All of the events in this book are fictional. All of the personalities here in are imaginary but in some very small way are vaguely based on actual people that I met during a six month tour in jail. All of the techniques used in this book, reportedly, work.

My portrayal of the police is brutal at times. Keep in mind, they live in a brutal world, so that you don't have to. Some say that the criminals are too graphic in this book. I believe that the public is sheltered from the true face of evil. If you wish to remain ignorant, this may not be a book for you.

Crime does not pay. When you are caught, and everyone is eventually caught, they take from you your most precious gift, freedom. Outlaws are criminals because of their total commitment to their personal freedom. In jail, they are in hell, irregardless of TV, libraries, three squares, and clean clothes.

Keep in mind, as you read this book, that if you too loved freedom as much as criminals, then you too would walk like a cheetah and have the eyes of a hawk. And you too, would end up as a caged animal, pacing your life away. In despair.

I

On the Waterfront, San Diego, California

Tomorrow

His eyes glinted as they darted back and forth and back again in the dark, gloomy bar. Sporadic rays of dusty light from the afternoon sun were the only illumination save a flickering neon Budweiser sign in the corner. Outside, the tropical sun glared on the pavement as waves of heat reflected on the dirty, flyblown windows. He gulped nervously at his scotch; the back of his fingernails clicking a staccato rhythm against the glass each time he heard a siren wailing in the distance. He tried to look cool, at ease, without a care in the world. He failed.

An attractive waitress in a white uniform, suddenly appeared at his side, out of the gloom, like an iceberg patiently searching for a ship.

"What's it going to be then, honey? Same thing, again?" He jumped slightly in his seat, startled. His eyes, instantly swiveled 90 degrees, and bored dead into the center of waitress's eyes like a double barreled shotgun. His eyes were black, so black that the pupils were just barely visible in his irises. Seeing the waitress, his eyes instantly softened and camouflaged their predatory nature. He smiled. He had a kind, seemingly genuine smile. He used it often, except with friends. With them, he let himself be who he really was. Well, at least he would, if he had any friends still left alive. He considered his smile as a weapon. Something to distract his prey, before he struck.

His foot touched, reassuringly, the valise under the table. 'Damn it to hell,' he cursed to himself, 'Gotta keep more alert, more on the ball, letting some no account girl of a waitress sneak up on me like that. Shit. This is when it counts. Can't make a mistake, now. Not now, damn it.'

His mind went back to that morning, playing and replaying the sequence of events. Over and over again, his mind stuck on a roller coaster that he couldn't get off, no matter how much he drank. Each round trip took a thousandth of a second, but seemed an eternity. He shook his head trying to knock the thoughts out of his head but invariability his mind was back on the action of the morning. It had certainly got screwed up, royally, fast.

"Yeah, girl, gimme another scotch. What the hell, make it a double. Where you from, anyway? Round here?" So how did it all get so screwed up anyway? Things were going so well, just as he had planned.

"No, honey," the waitress said, "I'm not from around here, I'm just working a while. Making me some traveling money. Then I'll be on the road again. You know how it is. Got the wandering in my veins. My blood just don't pulse right lessen it be a traveling. What about you?"

She looked at him in a friendly, happy way trying to guess how much of a tipper he was. 'He is kinda cute, in a hunky kind of way,' she thought, a little thrill radiated from her belly as she looked at him. Then she looked a little deeper into his black on black eyes and gave a little shudder. Luckily, she had gathered a lifetime of experience in just a few years on the road.

'Not now, girl, not now. And not him.' She gave her tongue a quick nip with her eye tooth to make herself remember. She had known men like him before. He would be exciting in bed but he would be cruel, he would enjoy hurting. And having hurt he would leave without a second glance or the slightest regret; leaving her to wonder why she made the effort in the first place, and to deal with her pain alone.

He watched as she walked away to get his drink. Her hips swayed gently as she strolled. 'Get your mind away from the skirts, Larry,' he thought to himself. 'I ain't got time for this. I've got to get out of this stupid mess, somehow. How the hell did it go wrong so quickly?'

It wasn't like he hadn't planned it. He had done his homework. Watched the store for two whole weeks running. He'd watched for the smallest variations. Watched for plain clothes store cops. He'd timed when that sissy, faggy assistant manager was on duty. Figured when the big security guard's days off were. Recorded each time a black and white had cruised by. He had even eaten cold hamburgers and stale, day old donuts, not wanting to miss anything. He had gotten himself a big piece of paper and wrote it all down, day by day, hour by hour. Figured out which day and what time was the magic moment; the moment when defenses were down, when attention was elsewhere and he could just waltz in and then dance out, tens of thousands of dollars richer. The hours he had put in, God, no wonder they called it a job!

Jobs. Yeah. He had real jobs before, good jobs. Damn good jobs. He hadn't always been a crook, hadn't always been on the con, hadn't always spent his life looking out for his main chance. He didn't mind working. He kind of liked it, actually. A physical job, especially. Felt good to use his muscles. To work as part of a team, to get something done and then look back with a quiet pride.

But taking stupid orders from fat, sadistic idiots; kowtowing to his mental and physical inferiors; not having any say in how he spent his working hours; that was no way for a man to live his life. A man had to have pride in himself or what does he become? An object of ridicule, an object of pity, a nothing, that's what.

He had put up with one good job for the money. He was unloading containers after they were lifted from ships. He liked it. Stacking different boxes on pallets just so. Making sure they didn't fall off. It was a job a man could take pride in. Then that stupid nerd of a supervisor had gotten in his face, telling him what to do, as if he didn't know, spittle flying out of the guy's mouth as he yelled, some of it landing on his shirt. Christ, he was the best man they had. He deserved respect, not this abuse, treating him like a nothing, like a man of no consequence. It was like the boss didn't care about the workers. They were just strong backs and weak brains, and if they weren't? If they had a brain and could think? Well, then, it was hassle time, my man.

So he had given the nerd of a supervisor a little, just a little, push. Just to back him off. Maybe stagger him a bit, let him know who he was dealing with. Let him know that this man wasn't just anyone. Certainly no one who could be messed with. Fucking A. And definitely, he wasn't someone who could be spit at. He had placed his finger tips against the guy's chest and just flicked them down. Nothing that would have bothered a real man. Hell, it wasn't his fault that the idiot had tripped on his shoelaces or whatever and fallen backwards off the loading dock. Lucky, the silly ass hadn't killed himself. But then blaming it on him! Hell, yeah, maybe he'd given him a little push. But not enough to make a real man fall. Fuck. Hell, with it. That was the end of that job. Had to leave the State when the bozo pressed charges. Shit. The world was full of crybabies. Talking like they were so tough and then just lying there on the ground, faking it, crying for the cops. Damn, man, anyone can talk tough if no one calls their bluff. That's what happens to a man without pride. Turns into a crybaby that just lies there when some innocent guy gives him a tiny, little push.

The waitress returned with his drink, stirring him from his reverie. She reached over his arm to place the scotch in front of him, briefly touching him with her left hip, causing him to smile.

'At least the girls were always on my side,' he thought, 'that is they are until I get tired of them.' He reached for his drink bringing it to his lips holding it between the second joint of his middle finger and just inside the joint of his thumb with the last knuckle of his pinkie supporting it on the bottom. He was very careful to never let the pads of his fingers or thumb touch the surface of any glass. It was second nature for him to never leave his fingerprints anywhere. He was so used to drinking in this way that he didn't even think about it as he raised the glass to his lips.

Lucy had helped him with this latest caper. He had looked for someone on the inside but man, oh man, he never dreamed of finding a looker like Lucy. She was down right gorgeous. Creamy blond hair that she wore long, to fly in the wind. Green eyes that sparkled out of a pixie face, and a body that just wouldn't quit. Legs so long, just made to wrap around a man. A cute butt almost over balanced by a great set of knockers. To top it off she had this grin that made a guy say, 'Oh what the hell! Let's have some fun!'

He didn't know what made the most beautiful girls like the wild kind of man. Maybe it was the danger; maybe it was the way he looked at them. Maybe it was the sex appeal. Maybe; whatever, who the hell gave a shit?

But that Lucy, man, she was something else. At first, he was just going for the registers and the cash box in the office. Then she got into the spirit of the thing and told him about how they didn't bank on weekends. They waited till Monday to count it up. They didn't bring it into the bank till noon on Monday. Two and a half days worth in one haul. And it was their own fault, too. Damn right. Leaving all that cash lying around. Asking for it, that's all it was. They could have used the drop box at the bank on Sunday. They should have. It was like they were daring someone to try to take it.

Well, if they thought that there weren't any red-blooded men still around in this world, then they sure thought wrong. And, hell yeah, red blooded women, too. Like that Lucy, man.

He took her out on a set up job, just to get some spending cash while he was doing his research. Something to put in his pocket, just in case he wanted to buy something. Sometimes he felt good walking into a joint, plopping down a pile of cash, just for a change, instead of coming around after hours and stealing it. He liked to see the clerk's face as he pulled out his wad, thicker than a woman's wrist.

And that Lucy, man. It was busy down at the airport, what with the holidays. He knew those lazy luggage guys wouldn't get all the suitcases up into the plane in time. They never did, always busy taking their union sanctioned breaks, and all. He and Lucy waited around outside the gates till he saw the luggage truck pull out. You would think that an airline would fly the left luggage to its destination when it missed the flight. Oh, no. That would have been too easy. Damn, fuckers. They trucked it across the country to save paying for another flight crew's wages and fuel for another plane. Cheap assholes. They deserved to be punished.

But that Lucy, man. She got out, and just as he told her, half tore her blouse off and lay kneeling in the street, long hair almost covering her bare breast, one hand on the ground holding her up, crying her little eyes out. After the luggage truck stopped, he sapped the driver and his helper just across the lower ear and left them in the bushes beside the road. Lucy jumped in the truck and followed him down a dirt road he had used before. The two of them tore through the luggage looking for anything good enough to fence.

Lucy loved it. The things they found. Really, you would think people would know better than to fly with incrementing evidence in their luggage. Lucy set herself up with a new wardrobe, slung five cameras around her neck and wanted Larry to take her picture with a sixth. It was a good score. The airline wasn't going to tell anyone that they had lost the luggage until they had to, the customers were the only ones who could identify they lost items. They wouldn't lose my it. The airline would cover the loss. He figured they had two, three days of complete freedom before the word got out on the street. Even at ten cents on the dollar, they made seven grand selling what they didn't want. It would have been a lot more but Lucy wanted all the high priced jewelry. He didn't mind. She had earned it. It was little wonder she was ready to bogie at the store. That girl was primed.

It was a big supermarket. They must take in a hundred grand a day, most of it in credit cards, unfortunately. They had ten checkout aisles all raking in the dough. He had her memorize her part in their little passion play and quizzed her like they were still in school. 'Thief's school', he thought with an inner laugh. She was quick and enthusiastic. It was going to be a great score. And it started out well.

He took a getaway car from his favorite used car lot, the airport long term parking, they painted each other up with make up. He put jungle tiger stripes across Lucy's face and down her throat and chest. She painted him with circles, stars around his eyes and a question mark down his nose. How they laughed. If only they knew then how it was all going to end up. They waltzed into the store Monday morning about eight. There were few customers, the tellers were open with their drawers full of money and the safe was right there waiting for him. Lucy locked the doors as they came in, something she used to do at the end of her shift, anyway. He bashed the security guard across the back of the head and cut the phone lines with wire snips. Lucy jumped onto a checkout counter and went into her act while he forced his way into the office, tossed everyone out and cut the phones there. Back in the store the few customers and the employees were hugging the floor as Lucy did her thing.

The way she looked, all fired up, as she stood on the counter one foot up on a cash register, short skirt hiked up, shouting for everyone to lie on the floor, face down. The fire coming out of her eyes, blazing out like liquid green lasers, as she swung her shotgun this way and that. Her hair flying around. What a natural! And she was really getting off on it, too. He could see her chest redden and her nostrils flare as the old hormones coursed through her veins. Her nipples erupted out of her great breasts and poked hard against her blouse. They strained against the silky material as she filled her lungs to yell and curse at everyone. And she was not the kind of girl who wore a bra. Man, oh, man, was she ever going to be good after, oh yeah! There is nothing, absolutely nothing, like a little crime and violence to get the old juices flowing. God, yeah!

Then that stupid little nerd of a joke of a mistake of an ass of an assistant manager screwed it all up. That idiot! Didn't he know the proper procedure in case of a robbery? Didn't he read his own rules for his own store, for Christ sake? Why didn't anyone do what they were supposed to do anymore? What's the world coming to? Oh, man. What a crock of shit.

He'd told Lucy not to get too close to anyone, to stay on top of her counter, to taunt and curse her old co-workers all she wanted but not to let them get a hand on her. She was having a ball. Telling some bitch to pull her skirt down. Told her she didn't want to see her ugly ass sticking in the air. Telling a pimply young kid to stop playing with himself. Yelling at a guy to roll over. She wanted to see his eyes as she shot him. Really getting off on it. A real natural. Born to kill.

Larry went from till to till shoving his gun in each checker's face and telling them to open their drawer. He grabbed the big bills, the twenties and tens then lifted the cash drawer out of the drawer, threw it on the ground, coins rolling, and lifted out the hundreds and fifties from where they kept them underneath. The money rolling around on the floor would distract the checkers and they would be so busy worrying about their bookkeeping that they would have less time to study his face, harder to give the cops his description until it was too late and he would be out of the city, gone like a mist on the wind.

He got to the cubicle of the office in the middle of the row of checkout stands and the manager shook his head when he was told to open the safe. Larry shoved his gun, he liked big guns for the scare factor, into the manager's mouth breaking a couple teeth in the process. The mark still refused, shaking his head. Larry pulled out his stiletto and pushed the point within an inch of the mark's left eye and then touched the tip to his eyeball. The manager's nerve broke and he quickly opened the safe.

Then that ass of an assistant manger jumped up, leaped over the office barrier, shoved his hand into the safe and ran with Sunday's money bag into the backroom. Where'd he think he was going, anyway? What, was he going to hide in the bathroom or something? Idiot. With a wild leap Lucy left her counter and ran after him, skidding on the floor as she landed. She caught up to him and snatched the money bag with a jerk and a curse, but then he grabbed the business end of the shotgun, wrestling for it, trying to pull it away from Lucy. Larry watched in horror as Lucy pulled the trigger and shot the nerd in the chest. The blast tore a hole right through him and out of his back, blood spraying in little droplets with a couple of bigger pieces plastered against the wall. The assistant manager fell and seized her with both hands around the ankle. She pumped shell after shell into his dead body and it jerked to the shotgun blasts, as he spasmodically tightened its grip around her ankle. He heard her in there shouting his name, crying for help.

"Get off me, let go of me, you goddamn asshole. Larry, help me. Get this guy off me," she screamed, panicked, as she emptied the gun into his back. Kicking him now, hammering his head with the stock of her empty shotgun. Swinging it like a baseball bat. Over and over again. The money bag jerked open as Lucy accidentally hit it with her gun. Half of the money went flying everywhere. Lucy tried to crawl back into the main store but the dead body had its death grip on her ankle and his dead weight was too much for her. They would have to cut his fingers off to get them off of her leg. Soon the sirens started and he got out of there. Fast.

"Damn, double shit, hell," he cursed to himself, "Accessory to murder. That is all I need. Stupid girl. And saying my name in front of witnesses. Ah, shit."

Still he got most of the safe and the registers and as for Lucy; the silly bitch should have done as she was told. If she got caught, that was her problem. Let her take the rap. Did she think that he would risk getting caught trying to save her? Him? Har. Har. Hah.

But wasn't she something up on that counter. That was something to file in the old brain cells, man. Some images last longer than others, to be called up in day dreams in dusty saloons. Lucy, man, he would take that memory all the way to the grave.

II

A Marina somewhere in San Diego Bay

Harv Benson sat on his boat with his legs dangling over the side when Old Sam, off the converted Tahiti ketch down on F dock, walked by. He watched Harv for awhile and then moved a few steps closer.

"You is doing that wrong, you know."

"Sam, what exactly do you think I am doing wrong?"

"You is putting that there tape around them there turnbuckles on backwards like. Supposed to put it on the other way around." Harv glanced up at Old Sam, looked back down and continued taping just as he had been doing.

"Why do you think putting tape on one way or the other makes the slightest bit of difference to the sea? It will hold or not depending on the tape's adhesive not it's applied orientation."

"Oh yeah, sure. Go ahead. Use them big college words. You still is doing it wrong. And now you going to take your lady and that there nice kid down to Mexico to get them killed off by bandits and by storms and all, what with your backwards tape and what ever else you is doing wrong on that there tupperware boat."

"The 'Rose Marie' is in fine shape, Sam. People sail down to Mexico all the time without getting killed or even slightly injured. Janet and Jill appreciate your concern, but we are sailing out tomorrow. And, in any case, just for your information, I am not putting this tape on wrong." Sam shifted his weight from one foot to the other, looking at the other boats, at the sky, at the wood of the dock. Finally he looked again at Harv.

"Well, I be coming to see you out. Give that bucket of yours a push, maybe. Your family, they can stay with me, you come to your senses. You knows, it just takes one little thing to sink you. Why, I remembers once way back in '67 or '69, I disremembers which, out in the Indian I was. Anyway, so there I was sailing along and all of a sudden a pin just popped out of a turnbuckle and my mast came tumbling down. Didn't have no warning or nothing. Maybe that's why I is picky about my tape. Anyways, by the time I got into Chagos two months later, I was drinking the antifreeze out of the engine's radiator." Sam tapped the toe of his boat shoe against a cleat a few times.

"Yeah, I knows all about the old blue eyed mistress out there. You can't trust her. No, sir, you just can't. She'll con you, she will. Makes you think everything is great and then, why, then she has you right there were she wants you. And she wants you dead. You listens to me. You youngsters think you knows everything, but you don't. You just don't. She won't be happy till you is on the bottom of the sea. You, your boat, and your family's bones all covered in seaweed, like.

"Just you stay in port. It be nice and safe. Maybe its a macho thing with you. Go by yourself, then. Your family can stay with me and take the aeroplane down to Cabo." Harv stopped for awhile, and put down his tools to watch Sam's virtuoso performance.

"Thanks, Sam," Harv said with genuine warmth. "You are a real gentleman of the sea. But we are all leaving tomorrow.

Together.   Janet, Jill, me and the 'Rose Marie'.   But, hey, thanks for worrying about us."

Not ten minutes after Old Sam had ambled back down the dock shaking his head over the follies of his fellow sailors, George Albright who owned the beautiful Peterson 44 in the slip next to the 'Rose Marie' stopped on the way to his boat.

"When you are finished there come on over and start on my boat, Harv. Can't let a good man be idle."

"Yeah, right, George. As if I don't have enough to do. I still have to fill up with diesel and get some Racor filters on board. You know that Mexican diesel." "Yeah. Actually the diesel isn't that bad. It is when they bring you the fuel in those 55 gallon drums and they don't dump the rainwater out first. But listen; leave a day later, a week later. What's the rush?" George fumbled around in his pockets until he found a cigarette and matches. "I got to give these things up one day but I just can't seem to do it. You know, Harv, you should be using rigging tape on those turnbuckles instead of electrician's tape. The adhesive is much more water resistant in rigging tape."

"What! What! Why can't I rig my own boat my own way? And why is everyone trying to talk me out of sailing to Mexico?" Harv put his tools down on the deck and glared at George.

"Harv, cool it now. Go if you want, knock yourself out with your tape anyway you want. I'm not trying to talk you out of anything.   But listen, we have a nice life in this marina. Good friends, great parties, stores are close, prices aren't too bad.   Why do you want to go and take chances out in the ocean? Did you read about that guy who was murdered down in Turtle Bay? He was anchored, minding his own business, when this teenager, for god's sake, goes on a rampage. He killed maybe ten, twelve people. Came aboard this guy's boat in the middle of the night and just started shooting.   Didn't even ask questions first.   Maybe he was just pissed off at gringos. Who knows?

"Why take chances with your family? Want to see Mexico? Fly down, stay in a fancy hotel, get a suntan and drink a margarita on the beach, like a normal American."

Harv picked up his tools again and holding them in his hands, replied, "George, do you realize that in the last week 15 people in this marina have tried to talk me out of sailing to Mexico.   What is going on?   I thought that sailors were an adventurous lot.   Ready to sail around the world on a whim, you know.   Just like that." Harv snapped his fingers. "It has been a really big disappointment. I thought that I was in the company of giants and they turned out to be mice hiding from their shadows." Harv went back to his work winding the tape around the turnbuckle ends and cotter pins.

"Yeah, well maybe. But no sense taking chances. That's what I always say." As he walked away, he glanced over his shoulder with a confused, scared look.

Harv was just finishing up on the turnbuckles when Alice from the big catamaran end tied down on B dock, smiled her way up the dock. Janet played bridge with her every Tuesday night. Harv had a premonition of where her amble would lead her. But he was not pleased when Alice proved him right by stopping in front of him and asking if Janet was aboard. 'At least she didn't complain about my rigging,' he thought sourly as Janet invited her down below for a cup of tea.

As he was finishing cleaning up on deck he heard Alice getting upset down below. The words pig-headed, stupid, ignorant and head-stuck-in-the-sand came reverberating up from below. Janet's gentle voice murmured in the background, calming.

Eventually Alice stormed up from below, anger in her eyes and sorrow on her lips.

"Oh, why do you have to leave?" she shouted at Harv. "Why don't you just stay here and live the good life? What is so wrong with staying safe and sound? Plus, next month they are going to put in HBO on all the docks. Why don't you just stay? Janet doesn't want to go, I know she doesn't. Not deep inside. A woman can tell. You just filled her up with stories of parties on the beach, drinking Pacifico in the moonlight. Well, you can drink Pacifico here and you don't get sand in your shoes either." Alice slowed down and gave Harv a chance to get a word in.

"Alice, we are going. Why don't you get your boat together and sail south, too? Think of all the great bridge games we could have on the sand! And if you don't like sand in your shoes, take 'em off!" Harv raised his eyebrow and gave her his best male superiority look. Alice stormed off rushing back to her boat.

"Amazing," Harv called down the companionway. "I think that was the first time I ever had the last word with Alice!" A double peal of girlish laughter echoed back up to him from the cozy cabin below.

He was putting his rigging tools away in the lazarette when a head jumped out of the main hatch. Blue eyes, framed by short blond tousled hair, beamed with joy.

"Hi, Daddy, whatcha doing? Mom says, that if you are just up here day dreaming that you are supposed to come down and have lunch but if you are doing something important then I am supposed to help you so that you get finished so we both can have our lunch before it gets cold and we have to feed it to the fish," Jill said all in one breath.

He gazed at her in total delight. She was rapidly, in the last few years, becoming the main reason for his existence. The happiness he had attained late in life was mostly due to a little ball of fluff who had grown into the second most wonderful creature on earth. She just had her ninth birthday and she had magically turned from a doll playing, secretive, little girl into a tomboy deluxe. Janet said that this tomboy phase was just that, a phase. Janet thought that Jill was reacting against her growing womanhood. Either way, six months ago she would hardly talk to him except if he entered her pretend world of tea parties and dolls, now; she wanted to help him fix the engine.

He smiled back at her, "Well, I can't keep you from your food. The way you charge around here, you have to get some feed in you before you run out of steam. Tell your Mom that I'm a coming."

"Yes, sir; Sir Daddy," she giggled and flashed her irrepressibly happy smile.

"Get going, punk. I can't get down the companionway with you standing in the way," he growled with a frown trying in vain to conceal his happiness.

Janet stood in her galley cooking lunch and realized she loved her boat. She had owned houses before and hated them. She thought that they were just expensive caves to sleep in. Every time she turned around she had to buy another something that had just broken. And the workmen! Just try to get a plumber, and then try to get another one to fix the first one's mistakes. Property taxes just kept getting higher, crime rate was soaring, and everything was going up except her happiness. Sure, she had friends. Lots of friends, but they were not the kind of friends who showed up when trouble came for a visit. But they were always there when she was throwing a party.

Once her apartment had been burglarized in the middle of the night. It was a terrible experience but now she treasured the memory as that was when she and Harv had gotten together.

She considered herself a light sleeper, but she never heard a thing when it happened. In the morning when she found her 36 inch TV, VCR, stereo, cameras, and CDs gone she almost went ballistic. Then when she found her jewelry missing she did. That meant that the burglar had been in her bedroom while she was sleeping.

She started to tremble and then to shake. To keep herself together she started calling up people, hoping that someone would come over and take care of her. She was a very liberated woman but right now she just wanted to be held, to be told that it was all right. She wanted to feel protected in a world that was suddenly a very dangerous place.

Everyone was very kind on the phone and wanted to hear all about it but no one offered to come over and Janet just somehow couldn't bring herself to ask. After all, if they were friends, they would just know, she reasoned. They would just know that she needed help, right now, and rush over to be with her. No one offered. By the tenth call, this one to an old lover and colleague, the news was out, and he knew all about the burglary from the grapevine. With nothing new to share, the conversation soon petered out with him saying how he had some important things to do.

Janet felt like throwing herself on her bed and kicking her heels in frustration like a teenager when she remembered putting the phone number of a sailor in her coat pocket.

She had met him walking along the harbor seawall as she liked doing sometimes when she was blue. She was throwing bread to seagulls in the water who were mostly ignoring her when he came rushing up the dock.

"Listen, do you mind? I'm in an awful bind. I've somehow managed to get the main halyard lost up in the rigging and it flipped around the starboard spreader and I can't get it down. What I need you to do is, but wait, excuse me, I'm sorry, sometimes I do go on so. What is your name?"

"Janet," she replied a bit breathlessly, taken in by his good looks and impetuous manner.

"Yes, well, Janet. Janet, if you could just wiggle the bitter end of the halyard, kind of flip it around, while I climb the mast, I would be ever so grateful. I would ask someone else, but everyone has gone off to the grand opening of a grocery store or a West Marine, or something and if I leave it much longer it will really get twisted up in the rigging."

With a laugh she followed him down the dock. He had to be harmless with a story like that. It was a little bit scary walking down the narrow dock. It looked like a concrete sidewalk but it was floating and it moved from side to side just a bit. She wanted to take his hand for balance but how could she? She didn't know the slightest thing about him.

"So what is your name? And do you always pick up women like this?" Despite herself, Janet blushed from embarrassment.

"Harv. But you can call me by my first name," he said, and then stopped speaking.

"Well, what is it?"

"Captain." They both laughed a bit at that.

"Here she is. The 'Rose Marie'." With an easy motion Harv grabbed hold of a shroud and swung himself on board. "Watch your step there. Here let me help you. Harv reached down, held her around the waist and physically lifted her up and over the rail depositing her lightly on deck.

Janet held on to him for a few extra seconds. She told herself it was just to get her balance but the two foremost emotions flashing through her body could not be ignored.

"Oh, god, what a hunk!" and "Please don't let me say something stupid."

She helped him rescue his halyard which turned out to be a rope that raised the sails. She wiggled the end of the rope he gave her for all she was worth as he shinnied up the mast and freed the tangle. Then he slid down the mast landing lightly in front of her on his toes and seemed ever so much like a big human, grinning cat.

"Can I offer you a cup of coffee or perhaps something stronger?" he asked her with one eyebrow raised in a piratical manner. He smiled, and every pore emanated charm and joy of life.

She agreed with a nod not trusting her voice to speak and he led her down below. It was a small boat. Janet thought it was a bit smaller than her bedroom. There were two single beds on either side with a table in the middle. Next to the door there was a really small kitchen about half the size of her house's already small bathroom. Up in the front there was another room and a bathroom.

"Welcome aboard, Janet. Have a seat and I'll make you up a special coffee right away. Sure, just sit there on the pilot berth. Do you like any special kind of music?" He quickly and efficiently started the stove with a special sparker, poured the water into the kettle, got the coffee and cups out and started a CD playing all without moving his feet. Everything was in arm's reach. He reached into a back locker and pulled out a bottle of rum.

"Do you care for a drop of the good stuff in your coffee, lassie? It will warm our bones on a windy day."

"But Harv, or Captain, or whatever," she said with a smile, "there isn't a breath of wind out there. It's dead calm." She held her shoulders a bit straighter, proud of herself for her nautical lore.

"Aye, Babe, but some days a bitter wind blows through our hearts and it takes a bit of friendship to light a stub of a candle in the window. A lot a girls wouldn't have come down to a strange man's boat to give him a hand. It shows that you have courage, it does."

She just smiled. And continued to smile for the rest of the day. They set up a date for the following day but she was sent to Dallas in an emergency at work. One thing followed another and they never did have that second date. Then she became involved with a doctor who turned out to be unemployed and a jerk, and then with a lawyer who was just a jerk. But somehow she never threw away Harv's phone number when she was cleaning up. She left it in the pocket of her sweater that she had worn that day. She thought of it as just a fond memory until the morning after she was burgled.

The phone rang about ten times before anyone answered.

"Yeah, who is it and what do you want?" A deep, gruff voice growled.

"Hello? This is Janet. Is Captain Harv there? Could I speak to him?"

A silence, then, "That is Harv off of the 'Rose Marie' you are talking about? The little boat down on C Dock."

"Yes, please. If it isn't too much trouble."

She held her breath and hoped.

"Life is full of trouble, missy," the voice growled. "This, here, is a pay phone. He will be awhile getting up here. Plus, I got to get down there. It may be a long time. You want to give me your number and have him call you back? It would be easier."

"If you don't mind, I'll just wait.   It is a bit of an emergency." It wasn't really, but Janet didn't know what her next move would be when she hung up. She had run out of people to call. She was at the end of her rope. She started to clean up the mess left by the burglars as she waited, reaching as far as the phone cord would let her. Finally, a deep voice emanated from the speaker.

"Hello, this is Harv." Suddenly she didn't know what to say. Maybe he had forgotten all about her. It had been over a month ago that they had met. What if he just hung up when he found out who it was? What if he didn't even remember her name?

"Hello, hello, anyone there?"

"Y-yes, h-hello. This is Janet. I-I helped you on your boat about a month ago untangling some ropes.   Do you remember?" she stammered. And then bit her lower lip waiting for his reply.

"Oh, sure. Hi, Janet. Has it been a month? Seems like last week. They said something about an emergency? I really rushed up here."

"Oh, I'm sorry, Harv. It's just that I don't know what to do and everything is a mess. They tore everything apart. Looking for money I guess."   Suddenly, she felt very foolish.   He probably had a girl friend, already. She was sure he had his own problems. He might even be married.

"You were burglarized? I'm so sorry. Listen do you want me to come over and help clean up? After all, you did help me untangle my halyard."

A sense of peace came over her and she felt that she could finally take a full, deep breath.

"Yes, please. Would you? That would be very kind."

_/)_/)_/)

He took her sailing out to Catalina Island.   There, anchored in a deserted cove with sea lions barking in the distance, they made love for the first time. It was as if they were made for each other. Within the year they were married and Janet moved onto the boat full time. It was so small, so much smaller than her apartment. Some of her treasures she put into storage but most she sold or gave away. She couldn't even bring a suitcase.   It seemed suitcases took too much space onboard a boat and wouldn't fit into any lockers.

She slowly came to see life differently through Harv's eyes. It didn't matter how much you had, if you didn't have happiness. Being able to watch a sunset with inner contentment was just as good as the joy felt when seeing a sunset for the first time. Happiness came from freedom, from the ability to do whatever you wanted to do when ever you wanted to do it. It seems that the rich are happy as they can afford to do expensive things that others can't, but they also have increasing social obligations. Harv said that living on a cruising boat was just about as close to heaven as people can get, here on earth. Plenty of freedom and no obligations, except, he said, to pretty little damsels in distress and to laughing fellow rovers.

Janet quickly made friends among the other liveaboards, the people who lived on their boats in the marina, full time. She found them very easy to get to know. Harv said it was because they were a transient people coming and going as they wished. Here today, gone tomorrow, make friends quickly because there may not be time for a long acquaintance. No one grilled her on her past and she was invited to all the parties just because she smiled and waved and acted friendly. No one wanted to know her politics or her religion. But they all wanted to know when she could come over for a cup of tea or for dinner.

After six months, Janet couldn't imagine ever living ashore again. Harv talked of sailing around the world; it was all just so romantic. Janet wished that her parents were still alive so she could brag about her new life. Still, every moment was so happy. Even shopping was a joy. Together the two of them would walk down the aisle inspecting each item to determine if it would be good on a boat. They could disagree, but it didn't matter. They both knew that as captain, Harv had the last say. And it released her in a totally unexpected way. Before, she had defended her independence with valor and feistiness, but now she wanted to use her feminine wiles to get her way. Instead of arguing for what she felt was right, she just smiled, looked deep into his eyes, let her finger tips just graze his arm, and said,

"Harv, I really like this one. Will you buy it for me?" He always did, with a smile on his lips, and in his eyes, that permeated his body. She believed her mother would have enjoyed hearing about her new boyfriend; hearing the happiness in her voice. Christmas and birthdays were easy on board. Harv had at least ten catalogs from different stores all loaded with gear, clothes and toys for boats. He had check marks next to the things he liked. He spent so much money on her. She just had to admire a piece of jewelry and the next day it would be on her pillow.

They were married on the foredeck of their boat with two other boats tied alongside to hold all the people. So many people! All friends from her new life. Her only surviving relative, her brother in New York couldn't come, work he said. But over a hundred new friends crowded on board the three boats and they all wanted to kiss her and to tell her what a lucky guy Harv was to get her. She smiled and laughed and her skin glowed like it was on fire and she was so happy she had to keep pinching herself to keep from fainting.

Married life brought a peace to her that she had never expected. Suddenly life seemed to make sense. Maybe she had found her destiny and was living it. Maybe she was doing what she was born to do.

Every morning she woke, with her eyes crinkled with happiness and a smile of anticipation on her lips. Every evening she fell asleep with a true hunk in her arms and joy pulsing in her heart.

For eighteen months they lived in paradise. Happy and pleased with each other. Then the baby came. She was a difficult baby. Difficult to carry and then a difficult birth. As a baby she cried endlessly and as a child, Jill was always so frightened, of everything. She would never be happy unless Janet was within eyesight. Jill would tolerate Harv but there was always a reserve, always her head was turned to locate Janet.

She was happy on the boat as long as it was tied to the dock. As soon as they cast off, Jill started crying. They tried anchoring in the harbor to get her used to being away from the dock. She eventually would stop crying but then would revert to sullen glances and total refusal to eat.

Harv talked less and less about sailing around the world. They were still happy but a bit of their former joy had dried up. Once Janet had gone shopping and Jill had fallen asleep in her car seat. Janet knew that she should wake her and take her into the store with her but Jill was sleeping so soundly that she just didn't have the heart; and she was so tired of all the crying. Instead she cracked open the windows and locked the doors and rushed into the store for a few quick items. She was only in the store for a few minutes, when the loudspeaker blared out,

"Will the owner of the Honda Civic, license number BXE 378 please return to their car."

'What the heck,' thought Janet? 'Maybe someone hit my car.' And she rushed out. A group of women surrounded the car and Jill was screaming her head off. A large solid woman accosted her as she rushed up to the car.

"Do you know that you can be thrown in jail for leaving a child in a car? That child might suffocate in there. I have half a mind to report you to the police." The woman stood in the way preventing Janet from getting to her child. The other women still stared in the windows. One was taping on the windows with a coin, which just made Jill cry louder. Janet lost her temper. It was just too much.

"You are an evil woman. You are all evil women. Scaring the poor little child. It is a good thing that the car was locked or you would have kidnapped my child, wouldn't you? She was sleeping when I left, what did you all do? Surround the car and tap on the windows until she woke up and then stand around like a flock of vultures waiting for the kill to die? Well, you all should run, not walk, to your church and fall on your knees and beg forgiveness from the savior. You are this close," Janet held her fingers up an inch apart, "to eternal damnation for the evil you have done here today. The Lord may forgive you but I never will. Now get out of here before I have you arrested for attempted kidnapping." With that Janet pushed the woman aside, opened the passenger door and scooped Jill to her breast, started the car and backed up so quickly that she almost hit one of the women.

It took weeks for Jill to recover.

When it came time for school all hell broke loose. Janet had to deliver her to the door of the school and then be waiting at the door at the end. Jill yelled, and cried all day long and drove her teacher crazy. The school counselor was no help. She said that some children are better able to cope than others. Some seem to take life in their stride, others find it too much of a challenge and recede into inner worlds and secret lives.

Then one day it all changed. Jill was seven and a half and she just stopped being frightened. Within a week she was climbing the mast to see if there were any bird nests on the spreaders. She hung out with her father and wanted to help him maintain the diesel engine. And she suddenly wanted to take sailing lessons with the other kids.

It was like a miracle. Harv started talking about sailing to Mexico and Janet started art classes at the local college which she could now go to by herself. When asked what had changed Jill just replied,

"Oh, Mom, I have always been this way." Janet was afraid to say anything. 'Let sleeping demons lie,' she told herself. And knocked on wood.

_/)_/)_/)

"OK, Sir Daddy," said Jill as she went down the companionway first, to where Janet had made a delicious meal of Thai green curry and coconut soup. She liked to make exotic meals from foreign parts. She hoped that it would instill the sense of adventure back into Harv, back to the way he was, when they first married. 'And now it was happening,' she thought with a secret smile, 'we are going to sail to Mexico.' A thrill of excitement radiated thru her. She hummed softly to herself as she washed the dishes after lunch. Harv dried them and put them away as they stood right next to one another, occasionally, almost by accident touching each other...

She had invited an old girlfriend to come and visit once. It showed Janet, just how much she had changed. It wasn't that long ago that she too lived in a big house with a mortgage had an expensive car and could conceive of no other way of life.

"But, Janet, it is so small," her friend had said. "You must live on top of each other." The boat gave a little lurch and Meg staggered then suddenly sat down on the settee. "Oh, you know what I mean," she said as Janet giggled. "There isn't enough room to swing a cat in here."
"Meg, I would much rather pet a cat than swing one. But you are right, it is very small. I'm not complaining though. I like having my man right where I not only can see him but can reach out and touch him; anytime I want. It's all about happiness, Meg. Back before I lived in my apartment in that house on Wilshire Street? Remember? That house didn't make me happy. It made my boss happy. I was a good little employee, bought and paid for. I had to keep working, to pay for my house. It made my parents happy, they thought I was on the path to happiness. It made the bank happy, they were

making a fortune off of me. But me? Being an accepted little worker bee never brought me any happiness."

"Now, I am my own woman with a great guy. We do what we want, how we want, when we want. And the hell with anyone who says we can't. I don't care if my boat is small. Freedom is the spice that makes living worth while. And the sex! Meg! The sex is so much better when you are free!"

"Well, it would drive me insane having someone so close all the time. You must be in love or something." She looked at Janet haughtily but her eyes turned green with envy. She left soon after, but Janet always remembered her look of envy.

Later that day, just before dusk, they walked down the dock to the shower block, a nightly ritual. It was much easier and cleaner to shower in the marina's facilities than in the tiny shower on board. Jill as usual was talking as they strolled past the many beautiful boats.

"My teacher was telling me that women are smarter than men because they have one big brain while men only have two little ones, that's because the right and left lobes of woman's brains have many, many, many, many more synapses or connections or something..."

Janet noticed that Harv was limping slightly. He had twisted his knee badly while playing soccer on the beach with Jill. He had gone from hard sand to soft while running at full speed down hill. He had never quite recovered from it and still limped when tired. Janet hoped that he would be all right on this trip down the Mexican coast.

"...that connect the thinking brain with the communicating side, Men don't, men can't think and talk and listen all at the same time like we can, we women are so..."

It had taken months for him to recover enough to walk without pain. The last thing that Janet wanted was for Harv to be in that kind of pain again. She would rather stay here and not go to Mexico if it would save him some pain. But he was so set on going. And the more anyone said anything about staying the more determined he was to go.

"...we are so much more talented, those poor men can just think or talk, they can't do both together, no wonder they need us women to take care of them, and..."

"Harv," Janet interrupted, "do you think we should take crew with us going down the coast? Someone to give us a hand with the grunt work?"

"Mom, I was talking, you always tell me not to interrupt, don't you? Anyway, I can do plenty of the grunt work, after all isn't my name, 'Button'?"

Harv had always wanted to buy a power anchor windless, preferably one with a deck switch or button. As Jill grew into her new personality and in size and strength, she had taken over the anchor raising duties. Now Harv would just call out "Button" and Jill would jump into action, race forward and haul up the anchor, hand over hand. Harv proudly called her his automatic winch wench.

"I don't know, Janet. It would mean giving up a lot of our privacy, having a stranger aboard. Besides, we don't really need anyone else do we? We have always managed in the past."

"OK, dear, just a passing thought. You know best." Janet replied with a practiced smile. 'Men,' she thought, 'they are always the last ones to admit that they might need help. Maybe Jill was right. Maybe women had more agile brains than men. Maybe they could see connections between things that men couldn't.' Janet had taken a degree in anthropology years ago and still thought of modern man as a product of the Cro-Magnon man that he once was. So many of the traits that mankind had developed back then were now important parts of mankind's personality. 'Maybe men needed simple, straightforward brains back then to deal with fighting saber toothed tigers and the like. Brains that found an answer quickly.'

"When you want something from Dad, you are supposed to say, 'Yes, sir; Sir Daddy.' that makes him really happy and he lets you get away with all kinds of stuff and eat candy before meals and get double popcorn at movies and pick what video to watch and, and, well, just about everything!"

"All right honey, I'll give it a try. Darling, sir; Sir Hubby, will you take an extra hand on board at least as far as Cabo, just in case? Please?"

"Sometimes you girls act as if I wasn't even here! Talking over my head as if I was deaf or something. What am I supposed to say now that I have heard your plans on how to hoodwink old Dad?"

"You are supposed to say, 'Yes,' to show how much you love us and then we can give you a great big kiss and then you give us an even bigger kiss and then you take us to the movies and buy us a double popcorn," Jill blurted in a rush, "and triple candy!"

"I don't think you girls deserve it, but I'll let you in on a secret. I put a sign on the bow not an hour ago. A sign saying 'Looking for crew as far as Cabo.'" Harv growled. "Now, Miss Women Have Smarter Brains, why didn't you see it? It couldn't possibly be that you were busy talking instead of observing, could it?"

"Oh, Sir Daddy Hubby, I love you so much!" Janet just looked at him with happy eyes that brought a sense of peace into his heart.

They reached the shower block and waved to each other as they went their separate ways. They didn't have the slightest idea that they were being observed from across the street by a very perceptive, slightly wild, definitely crazed, pair of eyes.

_/)_/)_/)

"So, honey, you want for me to freshen your scotch?"

He had lost track of how many drinks he had. Not that it mattered. He had a head like a rock. He never lost control. Not him. Never. It was just that those sirens that kept blaring as they swept past the bar. He knew that they were looking for him. He sniffed the air like a wild animal as if he could smell danger. He knew that they were out to get him. And why? Just cuz some floozy lost control? Hell. Out of the corner of his eye he saw the waitress waiting.

"What do you want?" he snapped.

"Listen, I don't have to put up with this. You want to drink in here ya gotta act real polite. Especially to me, being as how I am a real lady. So, anyway, ya want another scotch or what?"

"Yeah, what the hell, gimme another. And, listen, sorry about snapping at you, babe. My mind was far away." As the waitress started to walk away, he called her back. "Hey, babe, a girl like you would know her way around this berg, right. And I know I'm right!"

"I get around, sure, so what."

"Well, the thing is that I'm kinda tired of always taking planes and trains and buses and the like. You know I travel a lot, business, you know, and I get tired of always the same thing? I mean how many planes can a guy take in his life? So

I'm thinking, maybe you know another way to split this town. Yeah? Just to be a bit different."

"You mean besides walking," laughed the waitress liking him a bit better and still trying for a tip. "There is always the harbor. Plenty of boats always coming and going. Hey, you aren't in any trouble with the law, are you? Cuz I don't want to get in any trouble. Makes me nervous being around troublemakers." Slowly she moved towards him till her hip was touching his arm again.

He looked up and gazed deep into her eyes. Slowly he reached out, took her wrist and stroked down the inside of her wrist with his index finger, starting high and ending with his finger nail very lightly scraping down the middle of her palm.

"How about I spend the night at your place, to protect you from any trouble, any criminals; what do you say, darling? You never know who is walking around free in this world. Do we have a date?"

She felt the warmth spreading out from her belly again. She wondered for the hundredth time what it was about her that made her attracted to the wrong kind of guy. As handsome and as well dressed as he was, all her street smarts were telling her to say no. Still, she hadn't had any company for a while. And it would, certainly be better than that idiot television.

He knew she was going to say yes when she didn't pull her hand away. Yeah, it was the wild side that attracted the chicks. Most of the regular straight guys he had met in his life couldn't pick up chicks and didn't know why. Women liked a bit of the animal in bed with them. They liked controlling something wild with what was between their legs. Must be that, or whatever. Who the hell gave a shit? A slight smile spread over his face as he thought about tonight and a light started to slowly glow deep in his black on black eyes.

III

Any Street in the United States

He was about 18, with long hair, and was on the thin side. The most noticeable thing about him was his blue eyes. So perceptive, so knowing as if he had somehow forced 50 years of living into 18. His parent's had thrown him out on his sixteenth birthday. Some birthday present. He couldn't really blame them. They had stuck by him when he was in juvenile detention. They had come to his trial when they tried him as an adult at 16. They told the judge he was a good boy. Then, they had come to see him the first few times that he had been confined to the mental hospital. It must have gotten to them. All the electric shock treatments. Seeing their own flesh and blood writhe and arch from head to toe as the shocks went through him. Seeing the blood pour from his ears and eyes and nose. Bodily fluids from everywhere else. Seeing him so loaded with experimental chemicals that he was hardly human. No, he couldn't blame his parents. They tried their best for their boy. It was the world that was at fault. And it was the world he blamed.

But he had fooled them all. They thought that after twenty treatments he wasn't a danger anymore. Hell, with all the chemicals they had shoved down his throat he shouldn't be. But he had kept his mind, well, some of it anyway. He looked normal, now. His hair had grown back where they had shaved it to attach the electrodes. Then they had released him. Needed the bed for a new crazy. Figured he was cured. Or at least tame.

Those wild eyes were now on the shower block. He had watched the old man, the woman and the chick go in and he was waiting for them to come out. That chick was something. Had to be 9 or 10. Just the age he liked 'em. Virgin. Untouched. All for him. He hadn't done a little girl for a long time now and he was ready. He was primed. They thought he was crazy before? They made him worse. He felt himself start to grow larger with the thought of blood and guts everywhere and her whimpers as she died.

The old man had come out and gone down the dock and then the woman came out and went back to her boat. Just like a chick,   spending hours in the shower, washing her secret places, getting it clean, just for him. She had to be alone now. He hadn't seen anyone else go in. His eyes started to glow and his thighs twitch as the adrenaline coursed through his body. He walked slowly over to the woman's entrance enjoying the drama, teasing himself. Telling himself that he might just let her live, knowing that he wouldn't.

But then just as he was at the entrance to the showers, she ruined it all by walking out. Adrenaline fueled rage flared through his veins and he shoved her back inside by putting one hand against her chest, right between her breasts, and pushed as hard as he could. He hardly seemed to put any effort into it but he sent her flying, landing on her backside and crashing against the far inside wall. The towel that was wrapped around her hair falling about her face, blinding her. He followed her into the shower room, removing his belt from his pants.

_/)_/)_/)

Larry had just come outside. He had pushed the door open with the base of his palms, keeping the pads of his fingers and thumb curled in. He stood inside the doorway for a minute looking carefully around for black and whites, for undercover dicks, for anyone who seemed to be paying attention to anyone.

Chances were that they had made Lucy talk by now. They just had too much on her. They would threaten her with the chair or some goddamn cop shit, if she wouldn't talk. A girl like that with so much life in her, she would fear the chair. Yeah, she would talk. Not that he blamed her. It was just who she was. God, that girl had so much life in her. So much, it just pored out her eyes in green waves.

Traffic was light and he had a good view of the marina across the street. It was just like the waitress had said. Damn, he didn't even know her name. Well, they had a date set up at 10 o'clock when she got off, he would find out then. Or not. Some girls liked it better if you stayed a stranger. They wanted it hard, they wanted it fast, they wanted it over and over, and then they wanted you gone.

As he watched the street, he saw a guy leave the drug store next door and jerk his way spasmodically across to the marina. A car barely missed him, the guy kicked at it, hitting the fender with his boot heel as it passed. 'A real weirdo,' Larry thought. Cities were full of them. People who just didn't fit in, who fell between the cracks, and who liked being in the cracks. He kept an eye on crackhead as he scanned the street, much as one would keep an eye on a rabid dog biting his tail, lost in his own world.

'Not like me,' Larry thought, 'scum.' Larry didn't view himself as living in the cracks. He thought of himself as a predator. He had stayed in school until his tenth year when he was thrown out on a weapons charge. 'As if a 22 caliber pistol is really a weapon,' Larry thought with a snort. Everyone else was carrying switchblades. He had just wanted a little insurance. 'Just some protection.'

But he did learn a little in school. He learned that animals all have things that they prey upon, and that other animals prey upon them in turn. Except man. He was at the top of the food chain. His instructor explained how predators actually kept an animal group healthy by eating the weaker animals. Without the predators the prey group would slowly get weaker and sicker and die out. That is why all animals are both prey and are predators. Except Man. A cow preys upon grass, a caterpillar preys upon leaves. Trees block the sun from grass beneath them that use water and nutrients the tree might otherwise absorb. Wolves prey on deer. But no one preyed upon man.

Larry watched the guy slowly spasm his way across the street and head for the toilets by the docks. 'If man had predators, they would sure eat up that guy first,' he thought with an inner laugh.

He watched the weirdo and saw him go in the women's toilet and throw a young girl coming out, back inside. He had a searing hatred of child abusers, a feeling shared with almost all of his criminal brethren. In prison, child abusers lasted about two weeks after their crime was known. Few lasted more than a month of constant abuse. A month of being thrown out of bed and having their heads jammed between the bars. A month of accidentally having exercise weights dropped across their throats. A month of having the pads of their toes eaten by rats on the floor at night because they weren't allowed to sleep in the bunks with the other cons. Larry debated crossing the street. He didn't want to expose himself. The police must have his description by now. But as he saw the crackhead take off his belt, he said to himself,

"Ah, the hell with it. Maybe I am this guy's predator." And in a couple of long strides he was across the street and through the women's door. The guy had the girl's head hard against the wall as he tore at her clothes. Her face was bulging and red from his belt twisted around her neck and across her mouth forcing her jaws apart. Her eyes were wide in fright and astonishment and as he came in he saw them sag in pain.

Larry came up behind the weirdo and grabbed his hair, fingers digging down to the roots and pulled back and down as roughly as he could, exposing his neck, his left hand coming down in a chop on the guy's unprotected throat, centered on his Adam's apple, paralyzing his thorax, freezing his throat so the fucker wouldn't be able to breathe. Caught by surprise the weirdo fell on his back, on the floor.

Larry knew that the guy had to be on something. Adrenaline, angel dust, speed, whatever. He wouldn't go down easy. So he immediately followed up on his attack, dropping his knee, hard into the guy's gut as he lay on his back on the floor and hitting him on the chin with the base of his palm as hard as he could as his head came up in response to his knee jab. He hit him again and again, always on the same spot, the point of the chin, always with the palm of his hand, the blows coming so fast, they seemed continuous. He was careful never to let his fingertips touch the weirdo's face fearing that the face's skin would retain fingertip impressions. He felt the scotch he had drunk drain from his system in the thrill of combat. He enjoyed the hitting, the not holding back, putting his natural born talents to use. Fighting was something he did well. Fighting was something he loved to do. Fighting was a part of who he was. He smiled to himself as the idiot's head bounced on the tile floor over and over as he hit it. 'Like a fucking punching bag,' he thought. He tired of the hitting and walked over to the girl where she lay, crumpled on the floor, one eye watching from behind her hands.

As he held out his hand to the girl, he looked back at the punk. He couldn't believe it when the guy started to get back up. Larry couldn't have known that the guy had so many shock treatments that he was almost immune to being hit. Larry circled around to the door cutting off any chance of flight. The nerd rushed over to the girl, picked up his belt tearing it off the girl's throat spinning her head around and started swinging it, buckle outwards. Larry had enough. He had spent some time in prison, sent up for a burglary he didn't commit; not that he wasn't guilt of other shit. In prison, if you don't fight you are everyone's plaything. If you don't fight effectively you are doomed to endless fights. Once you start swinging, you don't stop until the other guy is flat on his back and unconscious or dead.

"Time to stop playing around, punk." He grabbed the belt as it swung around and pulled the creep towards him thrusting his first two fingers deep into the asshole's eyes. The creep fell back and Larry pulled his fingers out of the sockets and dug them as deep as he could into the fucker's nostrils and pull up, ripping parallel slits from his nostrils to the corners of his eyes. Blood pored from his face and the creep fell back and crawled away.

"That'll keep him quiet for a while," Larry thought as he grabbed some toilet paper to wipe the gunk off his hand. Then turned to the girl and ever so gently pulled her ruined clothes up around her shoulders. She fell into his arms, crying and sobbing with relief and horror. He saw the jerk run out of the door holding his ruined bloody face, trying to push one eye back into the socket.

"Where is your home?" he asked her. "I'll take you there. You'll be safe with me. Listen, we better get out of here in case that scum has any friends." The girl just lay there peeking with terrified eyes from behind her arms.

'The last thing I need,' Larry thought, 'is to hang around here till the cops come. Shit. I need to get under cover. The pigs would just love to get me now. Plus, that asshole will probably go crying to the cops, too. What a world. A regular guy can't even walk down the street without getting hassled by the goddamn cops.'

"Come on, girl," he said. "He is long gone now. Get up and I'll take you home." He reached down and gently pulled her up with a hand under each upper arm. Her frightened eyes just stared at him and through him. She was trembling so badly that Larry's hands shook with her. 'Wouldn't take much for her to go into shock.' Larry thought.

"Do you know where your home is."

She nodded slowly, her neck hurting, and turned to walk out the door. At the entrance she slowed to a stop and looked out fearfully. He gently took her hand and started to lead her out. He turned his head and waited until she looked him in the eyes, then while willing his strength into her, pouring his will in to her from his eyes to hers, said in a low, calm voice,

"You will be all right with me," and then "Time to go home," a pause and then, he reached down inside of himself for

35

all the strength he had and pored it out of his dark, black, double barreled shotgun eyes, and said "You will always be safe with me." Some how reassured, she nodded and gave him a little smile.

She led the way down the dock to her boat never letting go of Larry's hand. Ten feet to go she ran from him and scrambled onboard crying, "Mommy, Daddy, Mommy, Daddy!"

Her mother met her at the companionway and enveloped Jill in her arms as Jill cried as if the world had ended.

Larry stood outside on the dock, uncertain if he should go onboard or not. As far as he knew, they might call the police and want him to identify the girl's attacker. Yeah, right. When would he ever learn to never help out? The only good deeds he ever did were only appreciated by him. He still heard the police sirens of the city wailing, but not too close now. He noticed a sign advertising for crew posted up on the bow. So the waitress was right. He could get out of here in a boat. At least he could if he could figure out how to drive one. How hard could the rest be? Most of the boats they had passed had steering wheels. Should be easy enough.

"Shit, accessory to murder, aggravated assault, armed robbery and grand theft all in one day. Christ, how did things get so fucked up?" he murmured to himself. He kicked at a cleat. He saw an old man amble down the dock heading right for him.

"Listen young fellow, if you are looking to go sailing that is not the boat to go on. Look at the way it is rigged! I mean would you put your rigging tape on backwards like that? And with a family and all. Just ain't right. It just ain't."

Larry saw an old man stooped with age but with lively eyes that were full of fun and laughter.

"So, youngster, if you would likes to see the way a boat should be rigged; then you come with me and see my 'Pagan'. I can tells you a thing or two about boats. Yep, that I can. Why I was sailing the seven seas before everyone else in these plastic boats even knew how to take a bath."

Larry still didn't see any activity on board the girl's boat except the sound of weeping so he followed the old man down the dock to an old wood boat with rust seeping out of the planks here and there.

"Come on aboard. Would you like a brewski? I brews 'em myself. Nothing to it really. The kit costs $7 and makes 30 quarts of beer. Good beer, too. None of those chemicals in it like store bought beer. Makes me really popular around here. Everyone stopping by for a beer."

Larry looked around the boat. He wasn't much of a sailor. He had played around with a rowboat on a lake once and he had been on an occasional ferry to get across a bay. But it looked comfortable enough. Kinda of like a small cabin or a big tent. Beds here and there and a galley, he guessed it was called, in one corner. A table with a assortment of paperbacks was in another corner. Empty beer bottles stood here and there, some at attention others fallen in battle. Clothes were scattered about, hanging over things.

"Nice boat you got here," Larry offered as he sipped at his beer. It wasn't bad. Strong, but he liked strong beer. He hoped he wasn't going to get sick from it, or from the air. A strange smell permeated the cabin.

"You betcha, guy. Why this little baby can make it around the world if she and I wanted to go. She is a Tahiti Ketch. Plenty of her class have done some mighty impressive sailing, let me tell you that. Don't see 'em around much likes you used to. Everyone buys plastic boats these days. Must think they are going to dock 'em in refrigerators. Not much good in a storm. No way. Why, back when I was a bit younger I took old 'Pagan' out on the ocean quite often. Yep, she and I get along. Two peas in a pod, that's us. Some says that we even smell alike. Me from the beer I drinks and Pagan from the beer she spills rocking at the dock. She may leak a bit, sure. But it is good healthy salt water. Keeps her timbers clean.

"By the by, everyone around here calls me Old Sam. Not that I am older than anyone else mind you. What do you go by youngster?"

"Volcano. Glad to meet you, Sam," said Larry."

"Well, Volcano, have another beer. Made a big batch of it for Christmas for a big party. But everyone got sick or something, anyways, no one came. Been having to drink it all meself. Leastwise, till you came along."

"So, Sam, are you going anywhere soon. On your boat, I mean, sailing. Or do you know of any other boats going, say, to Mexico or some place exotic?"

"Well, Youngster. I was thinking of going off to Hawaii this year but I still got a lot of things to fix up on old 'Pagan'. Me rigging needs work. Not that it is bad or anything, you knows. But the Ocean is an unforgiving place. She'll eat you for breakfast and still be hungry come lunch time."

"How about some other boat. Anyone around here going sailing, anywhere?"

"No, not really. Less you counts that 'Rose Marie'. Going to Mexico or somewheres tomorrow, to hear him talk. You wouldn't want ta set sail on her though. Not seaworthy in my opinion. She'll break up in the first bit of weather that comes her way, that she will. She's jest one of them plastic fiberglass soulless boats. Course lots of stinkpots are going here and there all the time. But, they don't count. Them contraptions don't even have a mast. Now how can you go to sea without a mast? Or sails or a decent keel? They ain't even boats. Not the way God meant boats to be."

"Where is the 'Rose Marie' docked, Sam? Just to see her, you know." He saw Sam face fall. "But I think you are right, Sam, she won't be seaworthy."

"Yeah, right." Sam gave him a disappointed look. "You goes to the end of the dock and turn left. She's the one with all the baggy wrinkle in the rigging. The one where's you was when I met ya."

"Yeah, I know the one. Has a young girl on it? Got it. Tell me Sam, not to change the subject or anything; are boats just like cars to drive? I mean, jump in, turn the key and get going?"

"Well, Volcano, it ain't so easy. They's all kind of switches ya got ta click. You ain't thinking of stealing me boat, are ya?"

"No, way. This beer is just making me talkative that's all," Larry replied with his little smile. "I don't know the front of a boat from the back. What do you do at night? Pull into a boat motel or something? They have those little tug boats out there to help you out, right? Those Little Toots?"

"Listen, Youngster. You is all alone out there. Ain't no one to help you out. At night, you just keep on sailing. Got's to keep a good watch, let me tell you. Them there ships are jest as likely to run you over if'n they even see you, which they mostly don't. They up there eating that ice cream or whatever instead of paying attention to the sea. And dem tug boats! They is close to port, and even if one was to help you, they gonna charge you so much, might have to sell the boat, just to pay the bill. No, Sir. The sea is likely to kill you, if'n you give it half a chance. Best you stay here, where it's safe."

"I hear you, Sam. But I would like to see the sea. Try out a sailboat. Go somewhere, far away. Far from here, anyway."

"That they can do, Volcano. Why, sailboats can take you around the world. I recalls one time me buddy disappeared from the dock next to me. Didn't see him for months. He finally pulled back into his slip. I asked him where he'd been. Said he got a craving for one of them pizzas made with pineapple. Figured Hawaii was the best place to gets one, so off he went. Didn't tell no one. Jest went. Took him 2 weeks ta get to Hawaii, and then hung around a bit to get a look at the place. Said it was worth it, too, that there pizza tasted real good, I guess. How's ya beer?"

"Getting a bit empty, Sam," Larry smiled. But if you give me another I might fall asleep right here."

"No problem. Here ye go. Get it inside of ya before it gets warm. Tastes better cold. You wants to sleep, why they's a bunk right there. Help yourself. I might have another beer or two meself." After he finished the next beer, Larry put his bottle down on the table firmly.

"Going for a walk, Sam. Be back after a bit. No need to wait up." With that he walked up the companionway and off the boat.

_/)_/)_/)

Jill sobbed for 20 minutes, uncontrollably. Harv remembered his daughter having crying fits., but nothing as hysterical as she was having now. Finally Jill was able to stop her cries long enough to get a few words out.

"Man. In the shower. H-h-hurt me."

As she raised her chin to talk, Harv could see her neck was red and the skin torn and oozing in a few places. In the corner of her mouth, the skin had been ripped back and was bleeding. He noticed for the first time, now that her mother had stopped hugging her, that her clothes were torn. Her blouse was torn down the front to her belly and she was holding up what little was left of the front of her pants.

With a curse he charged out of the cabin and raced up the dock. The showers looked empty but just to make sure he ran into the woman's side. He checked out each cubicle, slamming open each door. No one was there. He checked twice to be sure. As he came out of the shower block a light blinded him. He put his hands up to his face to protect his eyes from the glare.

"All right. Hands behind your head. Turn and face the wall. Spread 'em. Move your legs apart, asshole. You have the right to remain silent. Anything you say, can and will be used against you in a court of law. You..."

"Wait, wait, wait," Harv shouted. "My daughter was just raped. In this shower. The guy must be around here somewhere. I'm trying to find him. You have to help me."

"...have the right to an attorney. If you cannot afford one the state will assign one to you."

"Listen. I live on a boat on this dock. I have done nothing wrong. Why are you arresting me?"

Another policeman came around the corner of the building.

"Let him talk, Jack. Maybe, he will hang himself. Maybe he has an explanation for what he was doing in the Ladies." He stopped behind Harv his truncheon in his right hand. He slapped his truncheon into the palm of his left hand over and over again, giving Harv his coldest look.

"We know your type, mister. Going around beating up the homeless. What was the matter? Did he step on your little pristine dock? Did he take a piss in your own private public toilet? Did you have to see the seamier side of life? We see it every day, mister. Welcome to reality. The Doc says that he will live. No thanks to you. He'll be blinded and disfigured for life, though. Cuz of what you did. For that, I hope that you get life, scumbag."

"No, no, what are you talking about. Listen, my daughter was up here and taking a shower when she was attacked! I'm trying to find the guy who did it. Listen, let's go talk to her. She is right down on the dock." Harv was still spread-eagled against the wall. He turned his head to try to look at the cop.

"Yeah, right. Pull the other leg. We know you were in the Ladies looking for more homeless to beat up. Or worse. Listen, we've heard it all before. Let the judge decide. We got us a collar. The captain will be pleased. By the time the newspapers pick up the story about the attack on this homeless guy, they will also have to report that we already have the suspect in custody. That is good police work."

"But I'm not the right person. I didn't do it. I have a, what do you call it, an alibi. I can prove that I didn't do it." Harv pushed himself off the wall and turned to face the cop.

"Up against the wall, you mother fucker. Who the fuck do you think you are?" With a violent shove the first cop threw Harv against the wall and the second hit him across the back of the knees with his night stick. Harv fell, his knees and elbows

40

grinding into the gravely ground, pieces of stone tore and lacerated his skin. The policeman continued talking as if nothing had happened. He put his foot across Harv's neck and pressed down.

"Hey, listen, perp. We heard it all before. What were you doing in a girl's shower anyway? Plus, you act like a perp, anyway, always yacking away at us. Trying to talk your way out of it. Giving us a hassle. Let's get him downtown. Then we can go wash our hands. And try to forget that scum like him exist. We did good, today. Real good."

_/)_/)_/)

Larry was walking along the dock looking at boats aiming towards the 'Rose Marie' when he saw the lights from a black and white up at the end of the dock. He turned and walked the other direction, careful to keep his face away from the street. He changed his walk, lowering one shoulder and walked on the outer part of the opposite foot. It changed him somehow from an aggressive young male into an older ageing man. Down the dock he saw an attractive woman in a bikini polishing her powerboat's rail in the fading light. He stopped, entranced, letting his eyes glide along her body, stopping momentarily at various interesting curves. He walked over to her and reached over the lifeline and rubbed the instep of her bare right foot. Startled, she lurched away.

"Sorry, you had some stuff on your foot. I didn't want you to track it all over your deck," he lied.

"Oh. You scared me. You sure move quietly. Usually people can't get near me with out me knowing it."

"I guess you were just too involved in your work. Wait a minute. You have something on your face." He reached over and rubbed an imaginary spot off her chin and then gently holding her face he leaned over and kissed her full on her mouth. He gathered his spirit inside his chest, in his lungs and in his heart, and then let it flow out his mouth and force it into her. Gently he reached over, touched her belly button with his thumb, his other fingers pointing down over the swell of her belly just above her bikini line and drew his strength, now hers, back out of her through his fingers tips as if completing a neural circuit. Electricity flowed between them and she closed her eyes with a gasp as her mind was lost in the moment. It was as if her brain disconnected and shut down; her body existing on automatic. She dropped her polishing rag at her feet. She held her face up ready to be kissed again, her mind a blank, her body afire. He stepped on board and led her, dazed and willing, down below.

He thought regretfully of the waitress. 'She would have been a lot of fun; in a lot of different ways.   Well, I'll just have to make do with what we have here. Besides, she is on the other side of that cop ridden shower block.'   He gazed down at the eager, pretty face below him, and smiled his little smile.

Once in the privacy of the boat, he removed the girl's clothes roughly, suddenly eager for her. Slowly the girl started to recover, realized what was happening to her, and started to struggle. He twisted his right hand in her hair and kissed her again willing himself into her, and drawing her back into himself with his fingers on her belly. She fell into a near comatose state. Helpless, her brain filled with sensation, filled with desire, blocking out any opportunity of thought, any thought of resistance. She felt only her body burning with concentric rings of desire, pulsating, widening and then centering deep, deep in side of her. Her pelvis thrust forward, her neck fell back, if her mind thought anything at all, it was only a non-vocal affirmation. Abandoning his hand on her belly, he forced one knee between her widening legs, put one hand on the small of her back, one hand twisted in the small hairs low on her neck, he opened his mouth wide and sucked the hollow of her throat below her chin, sucking any will left to her, sucking all resistance out of her.

And he did, everything, he wanted, to her.

IV

Somewhere in San Diego Everyday

The cops had shoved Harv into a holding pen and left him there. He had asked to make a phone call, but was told he had to be charged with a crime before he would merit a call. He asked when he was to be charged. The big cop just looked at him evilly and said that they were still adding up the potential crimes he had broken. And that if he continued yakking away, he would add disturbing the peace.

Four other men were with him in the cell. Two were obviously drunks and were sleeping it off, snoring loudly. The third stood in a corner and kicked endlessly at the bars. The fourth, a fairly well dressed man in a suit and a red tie, smiled hesitantly at him and then went back to staring at the walls. The stink was bad. It emanated from the broken and full toilet in the middle of the cell, exposed to every eye. Harv hoped he wouldn't have to use it, with everyone watching. Two ancient yellow lights behind heavy mesh wire were the only illumination. The guy in the corner kicking at the walls, stopped suddenly and lurched over to the bars and started to piss outside the cage. A big burly cop rushed over and with out a word pulled out a cattle prod and zapped the guy on the balls. The guy fell on his back screaming, piss still squirting out of him, straight up, falling back all over himself.

After dope head's screaming subsided into moans, the well dressed man walked over to Harv, carefully avoiding the spreading puddle.

"You would think they would put those animals in a different cell than us, wouldn't you?" Harv stared at him at a loss for words. "What are you in for anyway?" Harv stilled stared. "Hey listen you can tell me. Don't have much else to do in here till morning. Less you want to take a chance and go to sleep? Not that I would advise that, not in here. Listen. Tell you what. Let's keep each other awake. It would be much safer. You don't want to know what happens to people who nod off in here. And you definitely don't want to find out."

"OK. Whatever. Anyway it is all a misunderstanding. They think that I beat up some homeless guy but I was on my boat all day!" The words came out of Harv in a rush almost as if a dam had broken.

"Yeah, well, those homeless dudes get on my nerves, too. Having to walk around them on the sidewalks that we pay taxes for. Opening up your front door in the morning and finding one on your porch and wrapped in your newspaper, too! Plus, most likely they pissed in it." He stared at the spreading puddle. "I think they all should be killed, exterminated, man!"

"They are j-j-just regular people down on their luck," Harv stuttered. "The cops should be looking for perverts that attack little girls in showers. Christ, my daughter was attacked and I was arrested for looking for her attacker. And they want me to stay in this marina! They think that this is a great life. Not a chance! I am out of here. I am definitely out of here. Mexico can't be as bad as this, no way."

"Listen, guy. No need to be nice in here. We all know the score. Trash like them may be down on their luck, maybe, but they like it in the sewers. They like being a drain on society. They should be in here, damn it, not us. God knows that they steal whatever they can every day. Maybe a homeless guy was the one who did your little girl."

"Just because they are poor doesn't make them criminals. Those police didn't even listen to what I had to say. They didn't even care!"

"Yeah, cops, man. Go figure. Cops do pretty much whatever they want to do. Think they are on the top of the food chain. Not like those homeless bums. I think we should torch them all while they are sleeping."

Harv just looked at him in disbelief and sat on a bench holding his head in his hands.

A few minutes later a cop looked in the door and the well dressed man nonchalantly, ever so slightly, shook his head.

V

A Marina in San Diego

Just after dawn Larry tired of his boat girl. He had gotten a bit of rest, in between times.   He carefully put her bikini bottoms back on her. 'Nothing like confusion in the ranks,' he thought with a grin. 'She'll wake up thinking it was the most fabulous dream in history.'   He gave her unconscious form a kiss on the back of the head and a slap on the rump. Then he went exploring.

He found the engine room behind a heavy steel door. Big engines, man! He looked around for a start button, found it and pushed it but nothing happened.   He backed out of the engine room and found the steering wheel. With a look of joy he found an ignition key just like in a car. But when he twisted it, nothing happened. With a curse he realized he was going to have to have help if he was going to escape by boat. He looked around for a glove box with an manual in it. Nothing. He guessed they didn't do manuals on boats, or else hid them really well so no one could steal the boat.

He jumped off the motor vessel, after looking around carefully, and walked down the docks. The black and white was gone but he was sure they had someone patrolling the area. That is just what cops do. The bastards never gave up. He kept an eagle eye on the street by the showers till he reached the 'Rose Marie. He knocked several times on the deck till a women put her head up through the hatch. "Hello, just stopped by to see how the little girl is. I'm the one who saved her in the shower," he smiled, his little smile.

Janet looked at him with skepticism and was about to brush him off when Jill raced up the forward hatch and launched herself into the man's arms.

"Oh, thank you, thank you so much. I was never so scarred in my whole life. Thank you so much for being there," she sobbed. Janet looked on in amazement. It was the most that Jill had said at one time since the attack.

"I'm sorry," Janet said, "I didn't realize that you were the hero who found her." Again Janet wished she knew where Harv had gone to. It just wasn't like him. He was so good at keeping in touch. This was a situation that called for a man, and here she was man-less.

"Mom! He didn't find me. He practically killed the weirdo who tried to get me. I wish you did kill him. I am going to have trouble sleeping for weeks! Maybe for months. Wait till all my girl friends hear what happened! They will be so jealous! I met a real hero! I was saved by a real hero! A real live handsome hero with a great smile!" Jill's sobbing was replaced with excitement and pride. Janet felt a rush of happiness burst in her. She was so afraid that Jill would go back into being the frightened little girl of 18 months ago. But here she was acting normal again, and all because of this guy.

"Jill, go below right now. You were very lucky to escape, thanks to Mister-"

"Adams, Ma'am, Larry Adams. Glad I was able to help out."

"Thanks to Mister Adams here. My husband isn't here right now, Mister Adams, but I guess you could have a cup of coffee in the cockpit. We certainly owe you that much."

"Oh, yes! Oh, yes! Please come. Please do. I'll make it in a jiffy. I know where everything is; I know where everything on this whole boat is; do you want sugar and milk?"

This boat seemed to rock slightly as Larry stepped on board. He wondered if he got seasick. In the cockpit, she called it, was a steering wheel with dials and gauges against the front wall with an ignition spot for a key, but no key. Larry wondered if he should wander up and down the marina till he found a boat with a key in the ignition, but then remembered the power boat that wouldn't start.

"Well, Mister Adams, welcome aboard, are you a sailor?" asked Janet.

"No, Ma'am, but I have spent the odd night on motor boats," Larry said with a smile.

"They are different, aren't they? More like a house, than a boat. The 'Rose Marie', here, is our home. She has everything aboard that a house has and more. Well, except for a washer and dryer."

Larry just smiled. He didn't believe in washing and drying clothes. When his clothes became dirty or he tired of them, he went into the nearest store, picked out an assortment of outfits, showed the fitting room clerk the number of clothes he had and went inside the cubicle. He put on a new set of clothes, hung up his old ones on the hanger, showed the clerk the same number of hangers he went in with and walked out of the store. In cases where they had security tags, he pulled out a vise grip he had borrowed from the hardware section and squeezed the tag till it released. If he really liked something with the new improved tags, he wore a big hat into the store and stuffed what he wanted into the hat. The monitors by the exits only measured shoulder high. They couldn't sense anything head high. Later he cut the tag off with a dremel tool.

"Do you want one or two cookies with your coffee? We have some really good coconut ones that we can't eat too many of at once because we have to save them for our passage down to Mexico so we can get some energy late at night on watch so we don't get hit by a ship or run aground on some damn reef."

"Jill, watch your language, and if front of a guest. Really Jill."

"But, Mom, that's what Daddy says. I'm just trying to be proper sailor," she stated with a straight back, direct gaze and a nautical toss of her curly hair. She gazed over to Larry and gave him her girlish impersonation of a piratical glare. Larry sputtered in his coffee and burst out laughing. "What are you doing here in our marina? Do you have a boat here or something," Jill asked.

"No, I don't know anything about boats, but I have always wanted to learn," Larry smiled again. "I was hoping I could find someone to teach me. Show me the ropes, I think it is called."

"I know everything, almost, about sailing. Why, I have been to junior sailing since I was 7. That's almost 2 years! That's a long time. Why, after that long I must know everything by now. Do you want to learn how to tie a bowline? I can tie a bowline one handed and blind folded. Want me to show you? I can tie lots of knots. Daddy says I'm the best sailor on this boat as I am always practicing. And,"

"Honey, slow down. I'm sure Mr. Adams knows how to tie knots, too. How is your coffee, Mr. Adams?"

"Delicious, but getting a bit cold. Could you warm it up, for me? I must say this cockpit is just so comfortable. I don't think I have ever been on this nice of a boat."

"You should see my room! I have it fixed up really nice with all my favorite posters and books! I do have to share it with boat stuff like sails and a spear gun and stuff."

"Guns?" asked Larry. He nudged the valise at his feet. "You tell me you have guns on board?"

"We don't have any guns, even our spear gun isn't a gun, it is a Hawaiian Sling. That means it has a big rubber band and you pull back on the spear and when you let go the rubber band makes it go forward. It is really hard to use cuz as soon as I start getting good at it, I am so cold I have to get out of the water; that is why I am so excited about going to Mexico. And…

"Jill, please, you are not sharing the conversation. Please, for the next ten minutes only talk when someone asks you a personal question.

"Really, Mr. Adams. About guns and the like. These are really questions you should be asking my husband. I really don't know what is keeping him. He is usually so good about phoning if he is delayed or stuck in traffic or has to work late. I really hope he is alright. He has been out all night." Janet wondered just for a second if Harv had shacked up with some strange woman. But then she shook her head in negation. 'Not my Harv. Not my man.' But her eyes still looked worried. 'At least he could have called,' she thought with a worried sigh. She thought about calling the hospitals, just in case, but she didn't feel he was hurt. If he was hurt, she would know, somehow.

VI

Anywhere in the United States

Someone kicked his shoe. He ignored it and pretended to be sleeping, his head still in his hands, his body freezing. It had been a long night. Addicts had been thrown in, their faces, arms, bodies bleeding, walking like zombies still in the throes of their bad fixes. Drunks came and then left as their wives or sweethearts posted their bail. He asked again and again when he could make a phone call. No one paid him any attention. The kick came again, hard, very hard.

"Hey, asshole, get up, you are being released."

Slowly he rose to his feet and followed the uniformed policeman out of the cell, through several sets of locked barred doors and sat on a hard backed chair in front of a old steel desk as he was instructed. He didn't show the slightest sign of independence. He had learned his lesson well. He signed papers as he was told to do. He knew he should read them first but they kept flipping them at him, one after another, a stubby finger pointing and a steely voice saying,

"Sign."

He just wanted to get back to his boat. Back to his world. Back to freedom. Out of this joint. If there was an opposite of freedom, it was incarceration. He had realized last night, that everything he held dear was precious only if he was free to enjoy them. He would hate it if Jill and Janet visited him in jail, half a man, not even a man, an animal in a cage. Pacing back and forth, full of energy but nothing to expend it against. Pacing till the force inside him ate his soul from within. Finally, he was finished with the forms and they gave him a manila envelope with his belt, wallet, watch and money inside.

"All right. Get out. There's the door. Leave. And better not let us catch you doing it next time, perp. Or you won't get off so lucky."

Outside of the jail, Harv blinked in the blinding sunlight. After the gloom of jail, his eyes were little prepared for the noontime sun. He walked over to a bus stop, but then counted the money in the envelope as he dumped it out into his hand, and murmured to himself.

"Hell, with this. I have got to get back to my boat, right now." He stepped into the street and flagged down a gypsy cab. As the cab was pulling up, he saw a police cruiser passing by. Harv slightly crouched and lowered his face. Then angry at himself, he stood up straight and glared at the cop car. "I have done nothing wrong. Why should I be afraid? Or subservient? Or anything but free and proud? What has happened to this country anyway?" he asked himself angrily. Angry mostly at himself for crouching, being defensive at the approach of the police.

The cab dropped him off by the shower block at the head of the dock. He eyed the showers warily as he paid off the cabbie. Harv stumbled down the dock. His clothes were filthy, his knees bleeding again from the wounds the cops caused when they dropped him onto the gravel, his face unshaven and his eyes gummy from lack of sleep. As he approached his boat he saw a strange, hard looking man, with alert, sharp eyes, sitting in his cockpit.

'Christ, another cop,' he thought. As he neared he realized that this man was different. He seemed friendly, he lacked the arrogance of the cops of last night. There was something though, something about him that said, "Watch out, danger." This man seemed more curious than anything else. He seemed to have the feel of a cop, though. He had a feeling about him that he had come to relate to cops. His eyes, his eyes were hooded, he guessed it was called. The man had his upper lids drooped over his eyes, like he was tired, or something, but under the lids, his black eyes were as fierce as an eagle's.

Janet rushed off the boat and ran down the dock as soon as she saw Harv approaching.

"Baby, where have you been all night. What happened to you? Oh, Harv, you look so tired."

"Who is that man on my boat?" he asked, ignoring Janet's welcoming arms.

"Oh, that is Larry."

"Larry, is it? Gone for one night and I have been replaced by Larry somebody. What is this world coming to."

"God, you are in a foul mood. Where have you been? Jail?" Harv just glared at her. "You were in jail? Oh, Harv what happened. Larry is the guy who saved Jill from that rapist last night. Larry said he was probably some homeless tramp strung out on dope. He beat him up before he could do anything worse to Jill, thank God."

The fog began to lift from Harv's brain. Of course.

'Well, if it cost me a night in hell to have my daughter's attacker half killed and her rescued, I guess it was worth the price,' he thought with a slowly relaxing mind. Nothing had happened to Jill, thank you sweet Jesus. The scowl left his face and he reached out and snaked an arm around her waist. He saw her nose wrinkle.

"Get me my shower things, will you Darling? And a clean change of clothes." He walked over to the rail of his boat as Janet rushed down below. He grabbed the rail as if it were a crutch and he a cripple. Or if it was his only connection to reality in a swirling, mindless world where he just discovered he no longer knew the rules.

A yell came from down below and a mini whirlwind erupted from the companionway, vaulted the rail and into Harv's arms.

"Oh, Daddy! I was so worried. Where did you go? How come you are so dirty? I had to sleep with Mom last night. She was so worried that I thought that she might have bad dreams! Don't ever go away again without telling us, OK?"

He gently touched the bruise marks on her neck and the rapidly healing cut in the corner of her mouth.

"How are you, Pumpkin. Have I told you today that I love you?"

"Boy, Dad, you sure are smelly! You should go take a shower! No." Her eyes lost their glow as she looked inward, remembering again her yesterday. "Wait a minute. I'll get a hose. You can shower right here. I'll help!"

"What would the neighbors say? Me, striping down, in public view."

"Do you know what would make me really happy, Dad? Really happy? Let's just go to Mexico right now. This very instant. I don't like this place anymore. I used to. But not now, not anymore."

"As soon as we possibly can, Jill. Just as soon as we can." And he petted her hair and hung on to both his boat and his daughter.

Harv, against his will, looked twice into the shower before going in. He wondered how Jill would handle it. If she would be able to overcome the trauma of yesterday. For sure, she would have to have reservations about undressing and bathing in this particular shower.

Who knew what emotional upheaval the poor girl would go through the rest of her life whenever she bathed. At least he could make sure that her trauma wasn't reinforced by re-visiting the scene of the crime. He made up his mind. They would leave as soon as he got back to the boat.

The stranger was still sitting in his cockpit when Harv returned from taking a long shower. The stink of the holding cell just stayed with him no matter how much he lathered. Finally he concluded that the smell was stuck in his nose, in his mind he guessed, not on his body. A parting gift from the guardians of society. He climbed over the lifeline and sat down next to Larry.

"Hey, listen, I haven't had a chance to thank you for saving my daughter. I don't know what would have happened if you hadn't come by. I hate to even think about it. Is there anything I can do for you? Money?"

"No, thanks for the offer, but I have enough money," he said with an inward smile. "What I would really like is to spend the night on board. You know. Get to know the girl I saved, a little."

"Unfortunately, we are leaving for Mexico in a couple of minutes. Or I would love to have you spend the night. Unless," He looked at Janet and she smiled back, agreeing. "Would you like to sail down to Mexico with us? Only to Ensenada. Would take one or two days at the most. Be easy to get back here, they got buses leaving for the border every hour."

"Oh, yes! Can he? Please, please, please. I would feel so much safer. Please, Sir Daddy. Please, Mr. Larry."

"How fast does your boat go, if you don't mind me asking?" Larry asked taking a sip of coffee.

"Well about five knots normally. Of course in bad weather a bit less, in good weather a bit more."

"And five knots is about, what fifty, sixty miles an hour?"

"Oh, no. Not even close. It is about 6 miles and hour. Sailboats don't get there fast but they get there in style."

'Hell's Bells,' thought Larry 'the cops could walk and get to Mexico ahead of me.' Then he thought about not being able to start the power boat. He thought about having to walk past the police at the border. He thought about walking past the showers.

"Hell, sure. I would love to go." He stuck out his hand and the two men shook hands. Harv was a little taken back at the strength of Larry's grip. His hand was like iron. It wasn't like he was squeezing hard. He didn't look all that strong. But his grip! Harv forced it into the back of his mind.

"How long will it take to get your luggage? Get your passport?"

"Got everything I need for a few days, right here," Larry said and nudged the valise at his feet.

"Alright, Janet turn all batteries to on. Jill get the dock lines." Harv reached down to the ignition key on the pedestal and the Westerbeke 4-154 fired into life.

As the engine warmed Harv checked the wind direction and mentally calculated how he would counteract the wind's force to safely leave the marina.

"Not too bad today," he called down to Janet. But you better stand by to fend off just in case. They have us crammed in here like sardines."

With a few fancy ship handling maneuvers, the 'Rose Marie' was under way for Mexico.

Once they got past the half sunken breakwater off North Island and into the deep ocean swells, adroit maneuvers were not much use. Everyone on board was feeling a little off color.

"Any chance of turning this crate around? Really, I would much rather walk to Mexico. What do you say, Harv? How about you get the girl here to drop me off on the beach? It is only right over there!"

"Larry, look at the swell break on the shore. You would be drowned. Tell you what," he looked over at Janet and Jill, neither of whom looked like they would enjoy spending a night at sea. "Tell you what. I think we should head on over to those islands and anchor. Those are the Isla Coronados, they belong to Mexico, so we will have succeeded at escaping from the evil civilization that locks up fathers for trying to help their kids. What do you say?"

Amid a chorus of agreement, Harv spun the wheel and two hours later the were anchored amidst sea lions, dolphins, and a vast array of beautiful fish.

Jill had the fishing line rigged in seconds and that night they dined on fresh caught yellow tail.

"Damn, if you women will pardon the expression, this is the life. Harv, I want to buy a boat just like you. I want to sail around with out having to ask anyone's permission. Like when we left. We just went! That is so awesome!"

"Well it isn't that easy. We had to get tourist cards, fishing licenses, lots of paperwork, Larry. It is a lot easier to take the airplane down to Cabo, probably cheaper too, considering the cost of diesel. Maybe in the old days, sailors could go where they wanted, when they wanted. Not anymore. If we were heading north, we would most likely have our own personal satellite checking on our progress and watching if we make any unusual stops. It isn't that free a world anymore. But if you ignore them, pretend they don't exist, this is the freest life there ever was!" Larry cast a wary eye towards the sky. He shook his head and looked around him.

'If these sailors think that Big Brother could ever keep up with me, they don't know shit,' he thought to himself.

Larry had never been a great swimmer. 'Never seen the need for it,' he would have said. He sat in the cockpit as the family frolicked in the cold water around the boat. He was sure that a Great White Shark was going to attack at any time. He couldn't see any fins or anything in the water, but that meant nothing. He had seen all those shark movies. He 'knew' how fast they could eat you up. He started to worry what would happen if the family was eaten up. Could he drive this boat to Mexico? He looked around. He saw some land off to the East, but he wasn't sure what land it was. He had watched carefully when Harv had started the boat when they left the marina. Before he turned the ignition key he had gone below and played with something in the engine room.

"Well, while they are all swimming and having a good time, it is time for a little research." Larry managed to open the engine room doors without breaking anything. "Damn, they really crowd everything in down here don't they?" There were wires and hoses and switches and relays everywhere. He looked around for labels or signs. Nothing.

"Shit, this is going to be harder than it looks." He heard them climbing up the stern so he quickly closed the engine room doors and stretched out on a settee pretending to sleep.

VII
Any Jail in America

Lucy sat on the floor hugging her aching body. Every muscle was groaning with its own separate pain. She huddled in the corner next to a very smelly john with used toilet paper littering every square of the once beige tile floor. The big butch woman strolled by and Lucy cowered deeper into the corner. The woman had kicked her every hour on the hour since they had been together in the cell.

At first Lucy had fought. The big woman seemed to like it when Lucy hit her. Once she got in a lucky shot and nailed the bitch right smack on the nose. The woman didn't even seem upset as she wiped the trickle of blood away. She did reach down and grab Lucy's nipples right thru the thin prison issue blouse, twisted and pulled Lucy straight up in the air. Lucy flailed away with her arms and the woman let go and then kicked Lucy in the ribs again as she fell on to the hard, cold floor. Her torso was now black and blue and it was painful to breathe. She learned to keep as far away as she could from the big bitch in the 5 foot by 8 foot cage.

When a guard strutted by, the bitch sat on her bunk with her head in her hands. As soon as the guard was gone, she went back to staring at the walls with pent up fury, hands clenching and sweat popping out of her forehead. Against her will, Lucy started to doze off and remembered again how it all started, yesterday.

She remembered how the assistant manager grabbed her around the ankle and how she fired shot after shot into him. God, what an animal! Now, she found out, now, after he was dead. She wondered briefly how he would have been in bed as she dragged his body into the meat department. She used the band saw they kept in there and carefully cut his fingers off her. She got out the back of the store just as the black and whites were coming in the front. She had enough time to stash the money still left in the bank bag just above the muffler on an old truck parked in the alley and then the cops had her. They bashed her around a bit, cuffed her, drove her down to the station and processed her, took her mug shot, took her prints, took her freedom. She did as she was told and it went like clockwork. The cops didn't bother her. In fact, they seemed to give her a little space. When a new cop came in the room she could hear them say in a quiet respectful tone,

"Murder one," and they would give her long looks out of the corners of their eyes. They took her out of the station in an armored bus and brought her to the local jail. That's where the trouble started. First, they strip searched her, including forcing their dirty fingers into the orifices between her legs as they held her, naked, face down on a heavy metal table. She could see scratched messages in the paint, inches from her tear blurred eyes.

"Kill all the Pigs." "Live free. Die in jail." "Fuck 'em, Fuck 'em all." "Please, somebody, make them stop. It hurts. Hurts too much." When they were finished with her they gave her some prison issue clothes and threw her into the cell with this huge, ugly, dirty, evil woman. And the kicking started and continued and continued.

The next day, 3 guards opened the door to the cell. They forced the big bitch into a corner with electric cattle prods and pulled Lucy out of there. They frog marched her into a small windowless room, barren save for a desk, a swivel chair and a stool bolted to the floor. They sat her on the stool and handcuffed her ankles to the floor, her wrists behind her back. After five minutes the door opened and a slim well dressed woman came in and gently lowered herself into the chair and smiled at Lucy.

"My name is Ann Roberts. I am the investigating officer for this case. I want you to tell me everything about the robbery and the murder." Lucy just stared at her, outwardly calm. Inwardly, her mind was in a turmoil. 'Shouldn't I ask for a lawyer?' 'Do they know about Larry?' 'Where is that guy, anyway?' 'Is he going to let me rot in here?' 'Should I say anything to this woman?' The thoughts raced through her mind.

"It will go easier on you, if you talk. But if you don't want to, no problem, you can stay as long as you want in Joy's cell." Lucy couldn't help herself.

"Joy? That thing is called, Joy?"

"Yes, a bit of a misnomer, I have to agree. Especially considering that we think she has killed over five women in here. Cruelly, sexually, and we can't prove a thing. The last, we can't even find. Personally I think Joy ate her. We couldn't even find any blood. The guards think she licked the cell floor clean of blood. All that was left was her clothes. Now, are you going to tell me all about it?"

"I'd like a lawyer, please. And I'd like him here before we proceed with this questioning."

"Well, if that is what you would like, of course, no problem." Ann got up stretched, smiled at Lucy, and let herself out the door. A guard soon came, unshackled her and led her out the door. Lucy soon realized where she was going. As the cell door slammed shut, she turned and with a gulp, stared into Joy's small, glazed, pig-like, manic eyes. Slowly Joy's mouth opened and her tongue licked her lips.

VIII
Every City in America

Police Lieutenant James Peterson looked in dismay at the paper work cascading off of his desk. He had asked to be transferred to the marine division because he was tired of the endless mill of paperwork that goes with police work and wanted to spend some time on the water. A Lieutenancy, in such a small division' was considered a fantastic plum for some one like him filling out the last two years of his twenty. But he really didn't expect the paper to grow into mountains.

One huge pile of forms was nothing but stolen boats or boats that the owner had reported stolen. Sometimes Peterson wondered just how many were secretly sold by the owners and reported stolen for the insurance. One of the things he hated about being on the thin blue line protecting society against chaos was that so often the very people he was protecting were crooked in some way. It made him wonder why he was risking his life. Or at least was. It was much quieter on the water than on the city streets.

Another pile was filled with all the assault cases on boats that downtown didn't want to bother with. Fist fights, knife fights, ramming resulting in bodily injury. Fishermen were responsible for the majority, live-aboards most of the rest.

When he interviewed the fishermen, they shut up and would never finger another fisherman. They solved their problems within their community even if it ended with death. The live-aboards told so many stories he found it impossible to separate fact from fiction. Instead, the two parties involved in the assault fingered and blamed each other, they also blamed everyone within sight as well as the city, the cops, the State and the President. Some of them were well educated and their arguments were well reasoned. They would be untouchable on the stand. It was useless to arrest them without a foolproof case. He would end up spending weeks testifying but without any convictions. He found himself solving no crimes, but adding to his list of open files daily.

"And this is a plum?" he growled to himself.

"What was that, Captainne?" asked his assistant, a young Chicano woman.

"Nothing, Maria. Just talking to myself. And I am only a lowly Lieutenant, not a Captain."

"Anything you say, Captainne."

"Whatever, Maria, whatever. Anything interesting in all this mess? Anything worth the time?"

"Sure, Captainne, lots. Dominica's boyfriend got into a big fight with Judy's brother. They both went to the hospital to get sewed up. They had to bribe someone to not report the knife wounds. I know you are going to ask who they bribed but I don't know and even if I did I couldn't tell you."

"Maria, you work for the Police. If you don't report these things, how do you expect anyone else to report them?"

"Captainne, no one wants you to investigate. The fishermen, they solve their own problemas. Just sit there, and collect your paycheck. That's what everyone does in the Marine Division. Collect the paycheck. It's what they call a free ride!"

"Yeah, I know what you are saying. I guess I am just used to being a cop. Used to solving crimes. I want my life to mean something, to be on the side of the angels, I guess. I know I'm outside of the main thrust of police work now, but it still feels good to be a little involved. You know what I mean? Now who did they bribe? There might be a reward in it for you."

"Captainne, I would tell you if I knew. It is my duty. I tell everybody that I have to tell, if I know. But, Captainne, my memory, I think it is because I work so many hours, it is not like it used to be when I was in the school. Back then, they had the recess. Recess is muy importante for the memory, Captainne."

"Whatever, Maria, whatever, let me know if something interesting comes in."

"Veridad, Captainne." And she made a mental note to herself that if an unattached, single, young, rich white woman came in she would be escorted straight in to the Captainne. He needed a busier home life.

She didn't know why the boss had never married. She felt that he would be happier if he had a good woman to tell him that he made her happy. Then, of course, that would make him happy. It was the way that the world worked. She always was amazed that people in the great and wonderful America who were so smart in so many ways didn't understand the first thing about how men and woman completed each other. How they needed each other to be happy.

"That's what the Patron needs. A good woman," she murmured to herself. She thought of Manuel, her husband, and felt a little shudder below her waist. "And that's what a woman needs, a good man."

_/)_/)_/)

"You've got to help me! No one else will. I called the Police and they just kept asking if I called for help or told him, no, or anything. But I just couldn't, don't you see? It was like I was in a trance or hypnotized or something. It wasn't like I had a choice. But it isn't me I'm calling about. You've got to help them. He isn't like he looks. He seems nice enough but he isn't. He is cruel and evil. He used me like, like a thing. He hurt me so badly and you know what? He didn't even seem to enjoy it. It was like he was bored, with nothing to do, or something, so he started pulling wings off of flies just to watch them squirm! Except the fly was me! And then he told me that he would make the 'Rose Marie' take him as crew on their trip to Mexico and I am so afraid of what he is going to do to those nice people. You have to help them! Help them. Not me!"

Lieutenant Peterson held the phone a little away from his ear as the woman started weeping. He thanked his old buddies down at headquarters mentally. Sure got a hysterical raped woman who didn't even say no and don't know what to do with her? Oh, tell her to call good old James. He doesn't have anything else to do except to sit around and collect his paycheck. It isn't like there was any possibility of a collar. Perpetrator had left the country. They are probably laughing about it now. Some buddies. Nevertheless he pulled a piece of paper out and dutifully wrote:

"Rose Marie"
Sailed to Mexico
Suspected rapist on board
When?
What kind of boat?
ID's?
Hey! You know the drill! The works!

"I am going to let you talk to our head investigator in these matters," he said into the phone to the weeping woman. "Hold on for a minute."

He walked over to Maria's desk, handed her his piece of paper and said,

"Line two. Good luck. I'm going to see if the coffee machine still works." As he walked out the door he heard Maria saying,

"It's OK, Chica. You can talk to me. Those hombres, they just think with what's between their legs. You know why? It's because they squirted all their brains out, that's why. Now you tell Maria everything and I write it down on my paper. Then we will find this dog and we will teach him why us policewomen wear these black boots.

"Now this afternoon you come down here and we make an identi-pic of this guy with the computer. OK, Chica?"

IX

The Pacific Ocean off Baja

Harv leaned against the starboard coaming steering with his foot braced against the spokes of the wheel. Larry sat against the rise of the cabin top on the bow. Janet was down below making a breakfast of toast and eggs. Jill had started her home schooling course. She had been grumpy at first with comments of 'who needs school' and 'I am going to be a beach bum when I grow up,' but now she was lounging on the foredeck next to Larry, reading her science book. It was a beautiful day. The wind was blowing ten to fifteen knots from the northwest. Little waves pushed the 'Rose Marie' on her way.

"Life doesn't get much better than this," Harv shouted at the top of his voice.

"Dad, do you know that you men really are the weaker sex?" Jill called from the foredeck. "Your little sperm die all the time trying to get to the egg but us women only need one egg and it never dies till we tell it to. Isn't that just great?"

"Well, if I am going to die, let it be a day like today. This is so awesome. We are free! Free to go where we want. Free to do anything we feel like. No bosses. No cops! No rapists! This is so great."

Janet handed up a cup of coffee from the galley below. She smiled at Harv, love gleaming from her eyes. She was dressed in a bikini bottom with an apron covering her front. Harv thought that he had never seen her look more fetching. She smiled again, gave her bottom a little shake and presented Harv with what she called her Mata Hari look, while looking over her shoulder. She raised her chin, lowered her eye lids and pouted her half open lips. Harv responded with a drawn out wolf whistle and swelled out his chest.

"If you two would stop acting like teenagers, the serious person on this boat might get some of her school work done. Isn't that right, Larry?"

Larry looked up in surprise from the valise he had been playing with between his outstretched feet. He had slept on a little bunk during the night. It had taken him 10 minutes to spot all their hidey holes. There was the World Atlas on a book shelf that was sold by Staples that was really a combination safe for cash and important papers. It was worthless. He could jimmy it open in under 2 seconds. There was a false shelf behind the cushion where he slept. It had a little wooden Washington Monument screwed into the wood. When no one was looking he twisted the carving and exposed a key hole to the homemade drop safe. It was a normal lock, easily opened with a small screwdriver and a filed down feeler gauge to push in the tumblers one at a time. In the galley he noted a spice rack. One spice bottle had its interior lined with construction paper; a dead give away. Larry just noted things from his berth and smiled. He wasn't going to have any trouble with these people at all. They had been at sea too long, or something, and salt water had gotten into their brains. They were going to be like putty in his hands. It was going to be fun.

"So, what does it say about the survival of the fittest in there?" Larry asked Jill, pointing at the book.

"When a better individual of the species comes along, better because of mutation of her genes, it gives her a better survival trait, she has more chance to pass on her genes to the descendents than other members of the tribe. Over time, the tribe will come to resemble her, share her genes, and be superior over other tribes in the area.

"That's what it says, but they forgot to add that women are always superior to men. That goes without saying, right, Larry?"

"Always believe in what you think. Don't let others decide what the world is like, think for yourself. That is what I believe."

"Of course, silly. That goes without saying. We only learn stuff in school so we know what to rebel against!"

"Nothing goes without saying. A man; a person," he nodded at her, "has to have his own creed. His own beliefs. His own standards. If you don't, you end up doing what others tell you is the right thing to do, for the rest of your life. And mostly they tell you to do stuff to help them out.

"Do you think that is the newest mutation around? The ability to convince others to do it your way?"

"Silly, you are describing women. You men always do what we tell you to do. You would be lost without our guiding hand."

"If you marry, little one, better pick a milk toast, wimp kind of guy. Real guys don't like being told what to do. And that is the living truth."

"Dad?" Jill called out. "Do you like Mom telling you what to do?"

"Your Dad always decides for all of us, Jill. Now come and eat, everyone." Jill busied herself packing up her books.

"What do they teach you in those books about freedom?"

"Well, we fought for it in the Revolutionary War, defended it in 1812. Since then, we have jumped into wars here and there, anywhere, taking the fight to the enemies of freedom before they get a chance to attack us, as if anyone would be so silly."

"We had 9/11, which still sounds like an inside job," interrupted Harv from the wheel. "I mean the one day in his entire life that Dick Cheney was personally in charge of air defense over the Eastern Seaboard. How did those jets get so far off their flight plans? Who elected Cheney to run air defense? Do they think we are idiots? I guess they do. We all went along with them.

"We had Iraq, Afghanistan, Panama, Grenada, Somalia, the Balkans, Vietnam, Korea. None of those countries attacked the United States. Maybe Iraq and Korea attacked friends of ours, but who elected us as policemen. No one asked me, that is for sure."

"What they teach us in the school about freedom," Jill stated with a firm look on her immature face. "is our nation is based on freedom. But whose freedom? Freedom to get killed for someone else? Freedom to ruin our economy to help people that don't what our help?"

"Damn, girl! Who pushed your button? I sure didn't learn stuff like that in school. But you are right. Freedom means being free to do stuff for yourself and just for yourself. Sometimes that means going and beating the hell out of some country that is annoying you if enough of your fellow citizens want to do the same, just for themselves. When our government starts doing things because they are the right thing to do, or because they think we should do it, then that isn't freedom. Freedom is doing what we, personally, want, when we want." Larry took a big breath but then Harv interrupted again.

"Look at Norway. Norway hasn't ever attacked anyone since the days of the Vikings. Why can't we be like Norway? They have one hell of a great economy."

They spent the day sailing along the coast of Mexico, talking politics, fishing, dolphin watching, eating, having a grand old time. They had fresh caught tuna for dinner, and watched the stars for dessert.

Janet slept in the cabin in the front, forepeak, he guessed it was called, while Jill slept in the little cuddy cabin in the stern. Harv steered all night sometimes singing sea chanties at the top of his voice till a squeaky voice asked him,

"Please, Sir Daddy, a girl has to sleep. Do you want me to be grumpy all day tomorrow? Do you want me to be grumpy right now? Please, Daddy."

Morning came in from the east, painting the sky with rosy hues. Little clouds floated in from the northwest. The ocean lost its dark gloomy look and revealed its bluish colors contrasting nicely with the sky. The small sailboat surfed down small waves as she neared the Harbor of Ensenada. Aboard the boat the Captain awoke the crew.

"Larry, I need your passport. I'm getting all the ship's papers together to clear into Mexico. We will have to clear with immigration, customs, port captain and police."

"Not a problem, guy," replied Larry with his little smile accented with suddenly dead eyes. He pulled his valise from under his pillow opened it up and pulled out a .22 pistol. He causally pointed the gun at Janet in the galley making breakfast. "What I want you to do, Harv, my man, is take this boat back out to sea and head south. We are not going anywhere that has any police or authorities."

Janet stood still, her mouth dropped in amazement, a sugar spoon forgotten in her hand. Harv, crouched slightly, as if he might rush Larry but then thought twice as he looked again at the gun pointed at Janet.

Jill peeked her head out from her stern cabin. "What's going on? Why are you all so quiet all of a sudden? Are you planning to play a trick on me?"

"Jill, stay in the stern cabin. Close the hatch and lock it. Do it right now," commanded Harv. With a rush Jill was out of the stern cabin and down the main companionway.

"What is going on? Oh," she squeaked as she caught sight of the gun pointed at her mother. Janet reached out and grabbed Jill around the waist and both of them sank onto the floor out of sight of Larry. Without a moment of hesitation, Larry swiveled the gun at Harv's head.

"You two girls are going to need a new husband and father if he doesn't start to listen." He dropped his tone an octave and snarled, "I always wanted to be a captain with two female crew to amuse me. I will shoot you and kill you, Harvey. I am wanted by the police. We are not. Not; do you hear me? We are not going into any city or town. Now get out there and turn this boat around." He aimed the pistol at the VHF radio and fired a single round into the set. A few sparks flew out of the entry hole and then the radio died with a loud crack. He aimed again at Harv who was staring in astonishment at the radio, his mouth open.

"Get out there and turn this crate around. Right now!" Slowly, as if in a daze, Harv climbed up the companionway ladder, he disconnected the auto-pilot, spun the wheel and jibed the sails on to the starboard tack. Larry walked over to the galley and pointed the gun at the two women wrapped in each others arms, shivering on the floor. "Get up, cook breakfast, make me some coffee. I am in command now. Do it or I will kill the girl."

Janet struggled to her feet and busied herself in the galley, not trusting herself to speak. Jill, released from her mother's arms, jumped up and stared at Larry.

"And here I thought you were some kind of hero. You sure fooled me. You are just another bad thing that has happened this last couple of days. You stink, stink, stink. I hope you die. I hope the police catch you and shoot you dead. This is our boat, not yours." Janet grabbed Jill and pulled her into her arms again. She gently pressed Jill's head into her chest and muffled her mouth against her breast. With one hand Janet continued to cook. A muffled sound came from Jill. "Bad, bad, bad."

Larry reached over the island counter with the sink in it and shoved the muzzle of the gun into the soft area just below and behind Janet's left ear.

"And no tricks or the girl dies. Understand?" Janet nodded not trusting herself to speak and still not looking at Larry. When the coffee was ready Janet placed it on the table keeping her eyes on the floor. "Jill," Larry commanded, "come here and take a sip of this." He held out the coffee cup. Jill took one look at her mother and put her hands on her hips.

"If you think I am going to put your slobbery cup any where near my mouth you are crazy. Why don't you just jump overboard before my Dad kills you; you, you cretin!"

"Honey, Honey. It is OK. He hasn't drunk from the cup yet. Go ahead and take a sip." Janet could feel the Rose Marie start to rock again as the boat lost the protection of Todos Santos Bay. The sun shining through the ports started to change as the boat slowly turned to the south. Jill took a small sip from the coffee cup and then in a sudden movement spat it out right into Larry's face. With a lurch, Larry reached out to grab her but with a quick jump Jill hopped back into her mother's embrace in the galley and glared at him from under Janet's arms.

Larry's eyes narrowed. He stood up, carefully placing his valise under the table, and walked towards the galley. He reached over the counter and took out all the knifes from the knife block and reaching outside he threw them overboard. The last knife, a big carving knife, he kept. He leaned in towards Janet and hissed in her ear as he twisted the knife in front of her eyes.

"I will stick this into your daughter's privates and open her up, cunt to throat, if you can't control her. I will cut off your nose, woman, I will cut off your man's balls. I am in charge. All of you will obey, if you want to live." His eyes, close up, were laced with red veins that seemed to pulsate as he spoke.

His gun he forced this time into Janet's throat at the apex of her jaw, and jerked it in to emphasize each word. Janet could feel the sight on the end of the barrel of the gun tear her skin and was shocked to wipe a few drops of blood from her neck.

He walked back to the table, grabbed his valise and climbed up into the cockpit. There he unzipped it and pulled out a small wad of bills. He waffled through it and then handed it to Harv.

"I am not pirating your boat. This is a hundred dollars. I'll give you ten times that much if you take me to a safe place with no problems from you and your family. If you give me trouble, I'll give you a hundred times the trouble you give me; the trouble I'll bring will be bad, very, very bad. I'm willing to give you a lot of money for a few days passage. What do you say, man." He shook the wad in front of Harv.

"You big bully! We don't want you or your dirty stolen money, we," the rest of Jill's comments were muffled as her mother again pressed her face against her breast.

"Where do you want to be dropped off?" asked Harv, trying to control the anger boiling just under the surface. His eyes stared at Larry with a hardness new to his face. His hands on the wheel were squeezing so hard they were white from lack of blood. His knees were slightly bent and from the corner of his eye he could see a winch handle sticking out of the big Lewmar jib sheet winch. He tried to estimate how long it would take to pull the handle out and swing the heavy stainless bar onto Larry's head. 'Too long,' he thought. 'Way too long.'

"Don't take the money, Dad. It's blood money. I bet someone died so he could steal that money. Don't help him, Dad."

Larry shot an irritated look down the companionway at Jill. His eyes narrowed a little as he thought about what to do.

"Where did you get that money, Larry?" Harv craned his neck to see inside the valise. There was a lot of money in there.

"The fuck you want to know? I'm making an offer. Take it, leave it. What the fuck. It's my money, that's all you have to know."

"I don't want to be accused of abetting a criminal. An armed criminal. Armed and by the looks, dangerous. If you got that money honestly, tell me, and we can work something out, maybe."

"Fucking nerd. You had your chance." Larry shoved the money back into his valise. "Now, you are going to do what I tell you to do, for free." Larry smiled a little smile at Harv. "All of you are going to do exactly what I tell you to do, or hell will come visiting."

X

San Diego Bay

She knocked on the door and hearing no answer, walked right in. She saw a small Chicano woman behind a desk with a computer and a mountain of paperwork. Three other desks were scattered here and there about the dingy room. A single closed door labeled Lieutenant was straight across from her.

"Hello, my name is Janney James and they told me to come here first. I'm supposed to try to identify my attacker. I forgot who I was supposed to see."

Maria saw a young, and she guessed in happier times, pretty, young woman with a spray of freckles across her nose. She was dressed smartly in a black dress with a grey scarf. Her hair was Californian; sun bleached brunette, full of natural highlights. She wore boat shoes, normal for the waterfront.

"Hola, Chiquita. Come and sit down. I am the one for you to see. We talked on the phone, no? We kick him in the balls, si? This, what I have here, is the machina for the making of the picture. Come, I help you. Sit in this place, here. OK. My name is Maria and I work for the Captainne who is a good man, so you are safe here.

"Don't worry about the bad man who hurt you. We going to kick him with our black boots, no? OK, now this

67

button, push him to get the outline of the face. There are many faces, no? Keep pushing till the picture on the screen, he looks like the outline of man that attacked you. OK? Good, now you push the one with the eyes and then the mouth. Keep pushing buttons. It doesn't show you the finished picture yet. First you must pick all the little buttons, then you can push the big button. I come back in five minutes and see if you have the question. OK?"

Janney pushed away at buttons and was a little frustrated that see couldn't see if she was making progress. If she pushed the entire face 'big button' nothing happened. She stuck a pink tongue out between her teeth as she concentrated. She had to complete all of the input data first before the computer would finalize its result. She selected curly black hair, ears close to the head, covered a little by his hair. His neck was strong as if he was a body builder at one time. His black eyes showed white almost all the way around the pupil and were close together. She selected high cheek bones, a thin mouth and a strong chin. Finally she was finished. She pushed the big button and was amazed that the handsome, familiar face with the same cruel mouth stared back out at her. It was her attacker.

"Maria, I have finished. Come and look," she said excitedly.

"He does not look like a nice person, Chiquita. I think, maybe, that you are lucky that you are not dead."

"Yes, but what about those poor people on the 'Rose Marie'? I hate to even think what he might do to that little girl. She is so young and he likes to hurt. You just don't understand. Of course, this man is not a nice person, he is not even a person, he is a monster set lose on this world he make us pay for our sins." She started to cry. Maria stared at Janney for a few seconds with concern.

"Hey, Janney James. Here in this office, we are lucky. We have a good man in charge. Right now, he is out looking for this bad man. He could have sent some of his men, but no, he is looking himself. He soon will be back. You must stay. When you meet the Captainne, then you will be able to sleep tonight in peace. Here, you sit in this chair and read these magazines. I will run this picture thru our little data base we have here in this computer. Later we will send it to the big computer after the Captainne signs the paper. OK, Senorita?"

Janney nodded and sat down, picked up a magazine and

closed her eyes. She sat there, breathing deep, relaxing, concentrating on creating a white light in her head in the back of her eyes and waited. She had been taught in a yoga class that fear is the soul killer, the horror of fear itself. Fear is what changed you, made you different when disaster struck. One might almost die, or suffer some physical disaster and still remain whole, sane, inside. But once the phobia of fear enters the arena; the terror of pain, the anxiety of it happening again, the nightmare of the unknown, the panic of fear itself, then the essence of what one is, somehow changes. The rape victim jumps or cowers at the approach of every man where before, she greeted life and men with joy and openness. The maimed, cringe from a physical act that they thought nothing of before. Those who fear, those that allow terror into their soul, or have fear forced into them, limit their existence to a sad and repetitive scenario of a life only half lived.

Janney struggled to sit still, to stop thinking of the past, to see only her white light, to let her mind relax, to relax the muscles of her neck and shoulders and back, to ignore the pain still pulsating from her breasts and anus. She struggled and only partially succeeded.

When she opened her eyes again, Maria came over and looked at her with concern mixed with pity.

"Janney, the man who attacked you is Volcano Williams. He is a very, very bad man. He uses people. He uses them and then when they are broken, he throws them away. You are very lucky to still be alive." Janney's eyes started to tear. She gave a brave little smile and then turned as the front door opened.

Lieutenant Peterson walked through the station and into his office. Maria tried to get his attention but he ignored her. He just wanted to sit down. Sit down, put his feet up, and take a deep breath. He really felt that he was ready to retire.

Police work had seemed so important when he was young. Every single day was important. He felt he could change the world, make it safer for civilization, make the world a better place for kids to grow up. Now he just wanted to sit down.

No matter how many crooks he put behind bars twice as many seemed to spring from some fault in the human psyche. Would he be able to say that he had made a difference on the day he retired? Would the world be a better place because of his 20 years of service? Or was the thin blue line fragmented and splintered? Or worse. So many of his fellow officers had strayed to the dark side. They were getting rich selling out the public they had sworn to protect. Were chaos and evil winning the battle in the streets and in the souls of men?

At best he hoped that he was part of a holding pattern, holding civilization safe, letting evil know that to get to civilization, it had to get past him. If it could.

"Captainne, the woman from the harbor, she is here and she wants to talk to you. Should I tell her to come in?" Maria stood in the doorway her head stuck in around the door.

"Maria, I really don't have the strength. It has been a hard day. Ask her to come back tomorrow, would you please?" Maria came in through the door and stood in front of the desk, she pivoted slightly, showing off her figure to get the maximum effect.

"Si, OK, Captainne, right away. Only she has been waiting for hours now. She only wants to meet you. Just for one minute. It would make her feel better, she would feel safer knowing that men like you are on the side of the good guys." She put one beautifully manicured hand on his desk, fingertips just touching, fingers straight.

"Please, please, Captainne, it would mean so much to her. She has heard of you from other people. Good things, Patron. It has been hard for her. If you could only see her for a minute. See her please, then, if you want, push the button and I will come and say you are needed for the meeting, si? She only needs a minute, Captainne. Just one minute." Maria inflated her lungs, turned slightly and smiled expectantly.

"All right, Maria. Show her in but, just for a minute. And please, I am just a Lieutenant." He found it hard to resist Maria when she really wanted something and pulled out all the stops.

"Si, Captainne. Gracias." Maria opened the door and ushered in an attractive, trim, petite woman.

Janney saw a dark haired man with a James Bond curl on his forehead and piercing dark brown eyes when she walked in the door. He was about 40 and dressed casually in a button down shirt and slacks. He saw a trim figured, mid 30's lady dressed eloquently. She had a black dress with a gray scarf which complemented her smoky gray eyes and her sun-bleached hair.

"Hello. Your secretary said that I had to stay here till I could meet you. I really don't know why. She insisted. I just came in to help identify a criminal. Sorry to take up your time. I'm sure you are busy." Peterson started to laugh.

"Looks like Maria has been playing matchmaker again. I think that she worries about me," he said with a smile. She liked his laugh. It was full and without pretense. His face lost its grim hardness when he laughed. He suddenly looked younger and fun to be around.

"Well, it was nice to meet you but I am sure that you are very busy so I'll just say goodbye." He liked her smile. It seemed genuine and full of life. There was something about her. Maybe her smile. Maybe the way she wore her clothes. Something that got his attention.

"Listen; will you do me a favor? If Maria has gone to all this trouble to set us up and we don't at least go to lunch, she is going to redouble her efforts to enhance my social life and drive me crazy."

"Why not get a new secretary if she is so much trouble?" she asked with laughter leaking out of the corners of her eyes.

"What? No way. This department is run by Maria. Without her, I would be lost. She lets me pretend that I am in charge but we both know that I am just responding to those calls that she tells me about. Who knows what is swept under the rug? Anyway, I certainly could not take time off to have lunch with you without Maria. So how about it anyway? Are you hungry?"

"All right, Captainne. That is what she calls you, isn't it? I guess it is my civic duty to obey the police." As they walked out the door Maria gave Peterson a thumbs up and a big proud grin.

He took Janney to the greasy spoon next to the docks, where the fish was good and the tables were private. They lingered over their meal for an hour, talking of their lives, their plans and their hopes and joys. He felt attracted to her because of her beauty and laughter. She thought that he was interested in her, not just her body, but her. He wasn't young. That seemed to add to the relationship. He could talk knowledgeably about so many different things. He had a viewpoint on many different topics but still seemed interested in what she thought too. As lunch hour faded into the distant past, he knew he had to get back to work.

She really wasn't interested in another relationship, another man. The last one, Volcano, brief as it was, could put her off men for life. But as she looked at his eyes, she told herself, 'Get back on that bike and try again, girl.'

"I would love to see you again, Janney. I have to get back to work. We have to continue looking for the perp that attacked you." She deflated a little as if she really didn't want to remember. "Listen, do you want to go out tonight, Janney?"

"Like on a date?" she asked, eyes sparkling.

"Absolutely. I want to see you again and I can't wait till tomorrow. How about it. Want to?"

"Sure thing. How should I dress?"

"Casually. Pick you up at seven. I am absolutely positively sure that Maria has your address!" The words flowing from his lips like syrup. He smiled at her and intertwined the little finger of his right hand with the index finger on her left as they walked back to the department.

Janney like to dress well. To dress sexy. She wasn't looking for action, she wasn't that interested in sex, but she like the feeling of power she had over men when she dressed a certain way. If she was just slumming it in jeans and an old sweater, she was ignored. But if she put on her face, her battle face she called it, dressed in a low cut, tailored dress, men flocked around her. No matter how many people were in line at the grocery store, she was given cuts by men in front of her. She never had to open a door. And if she didn't like the look of someone, a flick of an eyebrow would crumble their self-confidence. And a slightly different flick would feel them with elation. She felt she could change the world, definitely her world, with just an eyebrow.

She decided to pull out the all the stops she could for the date and still be casual. It had been a long time between men, if you didn't count that Volcano creature. He didn't care what clothes she wore. He just wanted to tear them off. He didn't care what she thought, only what was between her legs. Nerd.

Peterson put Janney's identi-pic on the wire and labeled it as an all points bulletin. Within an hour he had replies coming in from everywhere. Downtown collaborated saying that a similar looking suspect was wanted for questioning about an armed robbery that occurred earlier on the same day that Janney was attacked. A uniform walking the streets confirmed that the same guy was reportedly seen in a bar in the vicinity of an assault at the marina showers.

Downtown confirmed that provisionally he was identified as being one Larry Williams, AKA Larry Adams, Stud Adams and Volcano Williams.

"You been a busy little boy, haven't you," said Peterson dangling the identi-pic from his fingers. "Busy little bees run into spider nets sooner or later." He tossed the picture onto the desk and put his feet up on the desk and on the picture. "Sooner or later." Then with a grunt he dropped his feet, stood up, felt to make sure he had his badge and his gun and walked out of the office.

Lieutenant Peterson walked down the dock to where the 'Rose Marie' had been berthed. She wasn't there, which they had already told him at the marina office. Still, it was nice to be out in the sun.

'Maybe I should take it easier, enjoy the sun, get ready for retirement,' he thought. He certainly had put in his time to earn his retirement. He had started out in a black and white in a tough part of town, East San Diego. Every night was filled with shootings and stabbings; every day was full of court appearances and paperwork. It was a good introduction to police work but he was very glad to say goodbye to it when he was promoted to a beat in Point Loma. There, he spent more time arresting drunk drivers and giving traffic tickets. He did get a bit of excitement with the occasional rape or burglary. A bit of excitement until he looked into the victim's eyes and saw what it cost them, personally, emotionally, to have been part the seamier side of life.

Berth 28 where the 'Rose Marie' had been was certainly empty. He asked himself again why he was here instead of sending one of his men. Again he mentally shrugged. Maybe he just had to pretend that he was a real cop again, that he was still on a beat. He saw an old man staring at him from the cockpit of an decrepit boat towards the end of the dock. He walked down and stopped in front of the old boat.

"I'd like to ask you a few questions, sir, if you don't mind."

"Are you a cop?" the old man asked with a gleam in his eye. Peterson loved talking to elderly people. They had nothing to do except to watch other people and they would always talk and maybe even tell the truth. Younger people turned off as soon as they learned that he was a policeman. And if they told him anything at all, it was likely to be an out and out lie or a half lie to get one of their enemies into trouble.

"Yes, sir. Lieutenant Peterson." He flashed his badge and asked, "Mind if I come aboard."

"Why, sure. Just watch your head on that there awning

pole. Hit meself on that darn thing must be five six time a day. You on duty or can ya drink a beer with me?"

"Duty, Sir. Do you know the Rose Marie? According to reports they left here recently and we are trying to determine if they took crew with them."

"You came to the right place then, cuz I knows all about Harv and Janet and their little girl. Seen her grow up right here in this marina. Yeah, they must have stayed here most on to ten year. Maybe eleven, don't quite recollect. Went to their wedding, I did. Big affair. Good beer. As far as the crew guy; don't know much about him. Liked my beer, so he can't be all bad. What has he done?" Sam asked with a gleam in his eye.

"Far as we know he hasn't committed any crimes. We are only making preliminary inquiries." Old Sam looked at the policeman in mild surprise. He knew he was getting old and that his mind didn't fire on all cylinders any more since he had taken up drinking full time, including breakfast, but he still knew that they didn't send any Lieutenant around making any preliminary inquires.

'What had that boy done,' he thought and cursed himself for not talking to him longer. He could have been the star witness. The hero. Maybe he still could if he played his cards right. He would be in the newspaper. Maybe they would give him some money or at least buy him some store bought beer.

"Well," Sam said craftily, "I could tell you a thing about him, too. Sat right here on my boat for the most of a whole day just talking and him telling me all about himself. Yep, I'm your man. Why, anything you might want to know, he probably told me. Guess you should take me down to the station in your fancy cop car and take my statement and all. Do I get to ride in front?"

"I think that a few questions here is all that is needed," Peterson replied. "Did he leave with the 'Rose Marie'? Did you personally see him on the boat as they left? Did you see him get on any other boats in this marina?" the Lieutenant asked mildly.

"Well, what I can say to you is he was sitting right here and asked me about Harv's boat. I told him all about it. About how it was a death trap and all. It be one of them there plastic refrigerator boats, you know. Anyways, he was all hot to go to Mexico or something. Tell you something else too. He was mighty careful what with that little suitcase of his. Always touching at it with his foot. Never went anywheres without he took it along with him. He's got something in there, you mark my word."

"Did you actually see him on the boat when it left?"

"I, er, I was busy about then so I didn't see them leave." Sam glanced suddenly at his refrigerator full of beer and then started to see his vision of fame disappearing. "And they didn't stop and say goodbye neither, think that they would. Only common courtesy." Peterson signed. Most of his conversations with liveaboards went in a similar vein. Fact and fiction and who knew which was which.

"That's fine, Sir. I'll get in touch if I need any thing more."

"Why don't you give me one of them there card things likes they does on TV so when I remembers somethings I can call you up." Peterson handed over a card with Maria's office number on it and carefully made his way off the boat and on to the dock.

He continued to walk along the docks heading for slip C28 where Janney's boat was. He wondered if she would be in. It was such a beautiful day. The kind you only get in Southern California. He found her boat, discovered that it was called 'Invictus' and knocked on the hull. No one was home. It didn't matter. He was happy just being on the water, or at least near it. The boat appeared to be in excellent condition. Janney must take very good care of it.

XI

At Sea Off Baja

Larry had rifled though the navigation desk, throwing things here and there. He had thrown overboard a couple knives he had found. Any possible weapon went over the side. He put a handheld VHF radio that he found in a locker into his valise. A flare gun that was in a little locker under a cushion in the cockpit joined the knifes in Davey Jones locker. While searching the cockpit he heard a loud zing. It sounded loud, dangerous and close. He pulled his pistol from his belt in a fraction of a second and aimed the gun right between Harv's eyes.

"Look, don't worry," said Harv. "It's a fish. It took our lure. I'll just pull it in." Harv walked past Larry trying to ignore the gun in his hand and started to fight the fish, pulling it in by pumping the rod and pulling in slack on the reel, working the fish closer and closer to the boat. He resented the lack of pleasure he was feeling. Usually catching a fish was a red letter event. Everyone would have been in high spirits at the thought of fresh fish and the joy of the struggle that all three of them shared in. Now, it was a hassle. And, it was his fault. He had allowed a stranger onto his boat. He should have said, no. A Captain is the boss of the boat. Responsible for everything and everybody. Now, his family was in the greatest danger of their lives because of his lack of self control. He had failed them. 'Well, that is going to change,' he thought, 'and I am going to have to be at the top of my game to get my family out of this trouble.'

Down below in her little aft cabin, Jill stared at her school books that her mother forced her to open. On a piece of paper she wrote, Kill. Kill. Kill. No prisoners. Kill the pirate. She drew pictures of knifes and poisons and slingshots and man eating sharks and lightning bolts. She still shuddered at night from the memory of that weirdo's hands on her in the shower. It had gone away while her 'savior' was on the boat, but now, now that he had shown his true black color, she had a hard time falling asleep. Her skin crawled at the memory of hands tearing at her clothes once more, of the belt forced between her jaws, tearing her lips. Of the belt choking her, of his hands grabbing, hurting, prying.

She knew it was her fault the pirate was on the boat. She was the one who had begged her father to let him into their home, onto the boat, a part of their crew, stuck with them at sea. She started to draw pictures of men dressed in black walking the plank.

Janet was cleaning up the mess Larry had left after throwing everything out of the navigation desk. She found a little Saint Jude icon that Harv and given her as she had struggled to learn to sail.

"Saint Jude is the patron of hopeless cases and sailors. Maybe you need some divine help to tell port from starboard!" Harv had said. How they had laughed. Their life together was so perfect; now it was being ruined and it was all her fault. She was the one who pressured Harv into taking crew. But how could she have known Jill's rescuer would be a desperate criminal?

'I just should have known,' that's all, she thought to herself. 'My woman's intuition should have told me.' She noticed that the St. Jude icon was cracked almost in half from being thrown on the floor. A tear leaked out of the corner of her left eye, and her pretty face faded into misery. Her hand grasped the icon, like it was a lifeboat and she pressed her hand to her breast as she cried silently, her other hand covering her eyes, her head hung in sorrow. 'It's my fault. I just should have known.'

Larry sat in the cockpit, enjoying the sun. He opened a few buttons on his shirt and looked about him like a king regarding his realm. He was escaping the cops, he was having an adventure, the wife was interesting, he was rich, and life was good, for the present. He sure had scored this time. He wondered if the little girl was right and he was a pirate.

'Pirate. Sounds romantic. Course, anyone else would call it kidnapping and grand theft auto, if this was a car. And I doubt if the god damn cops could make the distinction,' he thought to himself. 'Asshole cops.' Every time a patrol car passed him on the streets he could feel their eyes lasering into him, judging him, watching him. "And it fucking makes my skin crawl, asshole cops," he murmured to himself. Even when he was in the chips, money pouring out of his pockets, riding around in limousines, he felt them judging him, safe inside their black cars.

He had been poor more often in his life than rich. It was because, he told himself, he liked to live large. Hell, if everyone had seen as much death and misery as he had, they wouldn't ever save any money. Death came so quickly, so very often, why save for a rainy day? Why not live while you have the chance? If you want to have a good time, then, damn, have the best time of your life. Anyway, odds are, if you really love to live, you ain't going to die in bed.

He told himself when he lay dying, he wanted to have some memories worth remembering. When the time came to go to hell, he wanted to die with a smile on his face, a smile instilled from a life lived fully.

"Damn right. When they lay me to rest, the world would sigh with relief. Course it won't be to rest that I will be going," he told the steering wheel. Smiling he spoke to the sky, "The old devil and me, we going to have a great time comparing notes."

He looked off to the left. Far off was the coast of Mexico. A new and exciting country. A brand new place to rob and loot. New women to explore. New food to eat. Life was so good. Life was so fucking great. He couldn't wait to see what might happen next.

"Better than the damn TV," he whispered to himself while gazing fondly at the valise between his feet. "Better than the movies

XII

The City of San Diego

Lieutenant Peterson snarled at the phone as if it was an enemy. 'Sure give me a problem but not the power to fix it,' he thought. 'Downtown is only worried about political problems. I guess people on boats don't vote.'

"Listen, Mike. We think we have a positive ID on this perp who raped the girl at the marina and he has a sheet as long as your arm. Might be the same guy who held up that supermarket with the murder one. All we want to do is fly down the Baja coast and look for the boat he might be on. The Mexican policia won't budge unless we can positively identify him and discover where he is. Then they will go and pick him up and we can start extradition proceedings. It won't take but a few hours and you have the plane just sitting there. Come on, Mike. Let's get us some bad guys!"

Maria listened to the Captainne shouting at the phone. He was a good man, much better than the scum that they usually send down to the marine division to retire. She had been here for eleven years now, she had outlasted five bosses, and he was the best of the bunch. Usually the scum they sent, showed up drunk if they showed up at all. But the Captainne, he didn't know how things worked down here. He still thought that he was part of downtown.

Peterson slammed down the phone with a snarl and an oath.

"Politics! I didn't join the force to be a politician. If I wanted to get into politics, I would have developed a taste for champagne instead of beer. Damn! Damn! Damn!"

"What is the problema, Captainne?"

"Ah, Maria. Sometimes I think I am doing the right thing by retiring early. No one wants to catch crooks, they just don't want to lose their jobs. The Department has a spotter plane just sitting at the airport but the Commissioner mentioned last week that he might want to go for a ride so it is just sitting there. Since last week! You would think someone would call up the Commissioner and ask him when he wants to go for his stupid ride. Maybe I will," he said with a sudden impish grin.

"Ah, no, Captainne." Maria looked frightened, suddenly. "The Patron, he fires people for disturbing him. He is not a nice man, that one. But, it is no problema. Judy's brother works on the 'Cristo' which is a big tuna clipper. And his friend is the pilot who flies the little helo-copter for the clipper, to look for the fish. I'm sure that he will take you for a little ride down the coast. He has to fly so many hours every week. Sometimes he takes us chicas down to Ensenada. He will do it because I will ask for you and after all, down here at the harbor we have to stick together. Because, veridad, everyone else is against us. Anyway, Captainne, why not call migration in Ensenada? The fishing boats, they usually check in there to do the formalities and to pick up supplies. There are many things in Mexico much cheaper than here in the Norte."

"Good idea, Maria, get them on the phone, right away."

_/)_/)_/)

They had Lucy in the interrogation room again. She had a huge black bruise on the side of her face. With her tongue, she felt a molar on the right side. She nodded slightly to herself. It was definitely loose. They had her ankles handcuffed to the floor and this time they weren't gentle when they closed them. Already she was starting to lose feeling in her toes. She breathed as shallow as she could. A full breath caused agony in her ribs and then a coughing fit which just hurt her ribs worse. After what seemed hours, Ann Roberts entered the room and sat down in the easy chair.

"Tell me about the robbery. Tell me everything. Start from the beginning. Don't leave anything out, no matter how little. Start."

Lucy looked up in misery. She still hadn't heard a word from Larry. Not a word. She had expected he would break her out, or at least come and see how she was doing, or at the very least send someone to relay a message. She felt so alone. So very alone.

With Larry, she had been happy. He never had doubts like a normal person. No matter what the situation he seemed to be able to decide what to do instantly. And the sex! God was the sex so good. Maybe it was just her, but she loved it when a man took control and took her whenever he wanted. His passion seemed to ignite her own. She never had to worry about being ready, he was able to turn her on with just a look.

Once they were in a park and he had pulled her behind a tree, lifted her dress up and took her. She thought she would die from embarrassment, but, my god, she came like she had never come before. He took her anywhere. In the elevator, on the beach, once even on the altar of a church. It was so beautiful as she lay on her back, her legs stretched up towards the stained glass windows. She was thinking that Jesus loved sinners, didn't he? He loved that Mary Magdalene, a lady of the night. Maybe he loved her, too. Then she felt herself start to come and she forgot all about Jesus as her back arched in ecstasy.

But where was that guy, now? Didn't he care about her. Did she mean so little to him that he could just walk away and forget her? She felt tears start to well up behind her eyes. She fought to be brave, to pretend to be brave.

"I repeat for the last time. Tell me everything about the robbery. Every last detail, everything! Of course, if you would rather return to Joy's cell?" Ann looked at Lucy like a bug on a stick, like a thing.

"May I please have a lawyer?"

"Absolutely. We will put the request in right away. You should be assigned one in about a week. No problem. I'll just have the guard return you to your cell." Lucy stared at Roberts in fear, lips trembling, eyes sunk into her lower eyelids, jaw loose. Roberts stared back, right into Lucy's eyes without blinking, without moving a muscle, as if she was made of stone.

"No. No. Alright. I'll tell you everything. Everything. But please, don't put me back in with Joy. Promise?"

"If you cooperate fully, hold nothing back, name names and are totally honest, I'll send you to the infirmary. If not, if you hold back even a little, just a little, well it looks like Joy has you tenderized, no doubt she will start eating soon."

'Ok, Ok, I will, I promise, really." Her eyes were pleading. The terror in them pouring out, filling the room in waves with the scent of her fear. The tears finally poured out of her and ran down her face.

"Start."

"I guess it all started at that biker's bar north of town, I really don't remember the name, really! I'm sorry, I just can't remember, I'm so sorry."

"Continue."

"I went with a couple of girl friends and I met this guy called 'Stud'. Only it later turned out his real name was Larry. Anyway, we hit it off and we ended up at his place. He must really have liked my looks as he zeroed in on me at the bar. Didn't even look at anyone else. He ignored my girl friends; I guess that should have been a warning. But he had the nicest smile.

"Anyway, we, we hung out together for a while then he came up with this idea to rob the store where I used to work. He gave me this shotgun. He, he said it was a realistic toy. He said I was going to be like an actress. He said I wasn't going to be myself. I was going to play the part of a hoodlum or a mol or something. Anyway, he made me stand up on top of a counter and watch everyone and make sure they stayed lying down. But then I started to have second thoughts. I thought I would run out the back entrance to get away. If he knew I was leaving, I'm sure he would have killed me. But as I was leaving, one of my old bosses tackled me. He, he tried to pull the toy gun away from me and it went off. I was so scared! He must have had his hand on the trigger as it fired over and over again. God, it was awful. Finally, I got away and got out the back service entrance and that is when your policemen rescued me."

Ann Roberts looked at her for a few minutes and then

pulled out an ident-sketch that had come off the wire. She slid the picture halfway across the table and watched Lucy's face.

"Is this the guy?"

"Yes!" she said with surprise. "That is him. Is he a wanted criminal? I must have been lucky to get away from him!"

Ann pushed over a baggie with what looked like severed fingers inside. She didn't say anything. Lucy continued to look at the ident-sketch ignoring the baggie.

"And these? Do you recognize these?"

"No, what are they? They look almost like, like fingers." Lucy's face had turned white but she smiled gamely at Ann Roberts.

"Huh, huh. These were found in the butcher shop of the supermarket by the band saw. The saw had your finger prints on it. Why do you think your prints were on the saw?"

Lucy looked scared, she closed her eyes thinking madly, and finally said, "I really don't know. I think I went in there on my last day of work, for something. I think it was a special order. That must be it. Yes, I remember now. The butcher needed someone to turn on the saw. So I did." She was really trying to be brave, now, but it wasn't working. She was just too scared.

"Unless, you can be more forthcoming I am afraid we will have to put you back in the cage with Joy. We have been watching Joy for a long time now, and we can tell when she is just being violent, and when she will really start to get weird. I understand that when she starts to eat her victims, she starts with the boobs and the eyeballs. The thing is, you are still living as she starts to eat your nose and your lips."

Lucy's face, if it had been white before now turned ashen. Her eyes turned up in their sockets and she fainted, falling onto the desk, her face next to the baggie of fingers.

Ann Roberts pulled out a note book and made a few notations and then pulled the evidence bag away from Lucy's face. With a sigh, she pulled opened a lower drawer, lifted out a black pistol, put her feet up on the corner of the desk and casually shot Lucy in the face.

XIII

Off the Coast of Baja

Larry had his gun stuck in his belt as he stood in the cockpit of the 'Rose Marie'. The wind whistled in his ears and blew his black hair around his face. The waves were bigger now and the occasional one turned into spray after it hit the stern and covered Larry's lower legs.

Next to him sat Janet, steering. The auto pilot was having trouble keeping up with the worsening conditions and required a helping hand now and then. Harv was sleeping after another hard night, down below. Jill was curled up beside him.

"I admire the way you can steer the boat, Janet," he said. "Is this a storm?"

"Not even a gale. The boat can take a whole lot more abuse than we ever can. But this is nothing. Sailors are a tough breed. Why? Are you getting seasick?"

"I don't think so. If fact, I have never been sick a day in my life, so I am sure I am not seasick. In fact, I am hungry. I could eat a horse. There, that shows I'm not sick, I think. Who is cooking today?"

"Everyone else is busy working the boat. Why don't you help yourself? There are some oranges and grapefruit and coke in the fridge, some chocolate bars in the locker just next to the fridge and Fritos on the table. Help yourself."

Janet thought, 'I hope all that rich food does make you sick, you rotten, excuse of a man.' Larry went down below and started stuffing his face with chocolate and chips. In fifteen minutes, he was back in the cockpit definitely looking greener.

"I don't feel all that good. I don't feel good at all." He stood in the companionway and swayed with the movement of the boat.

"Here, sit down on the lee side and watch the waves. That will make you feel better. Don't look at the horizon. That is the worse thing you can do. Best thing is to eat some more of those greasy chips and drink that coke. That will settle your stomach. If that doesn't work, I better get you some pills." She pasted a concerned look on her face and forced her voice to sound low and worried.

"Get me those pills right now, hurry. I think something is wrong with these chips. Get them now, damn it. Hurry." Janet rushed down below. She felt the auto pilot start to lose it again but she didn't care. Maybe that bastard would be washed overboard. In the forward head she reached for the Dramamine and hesitated. Just behind the Dramamine was a bottle of Valium. Quickly she emptied out the Dramamine and shook in the ten pills of Valium left in the bottle into the Dramamine container. She grabbed the vial and rushed back on deck.

The 'Rose Marie' had turned sideways to the waves. The sails were luffing madly, shaking the boat, the waves were crashing over the side of the boat. The auto-helm was squealing away as it tried to correct the course. Janet reached out and spun the wheel as hard as she could. Slowly the boat came back on its course away from the waves and wind. Janet quickly scanned the rig for signs of damage. Seeing none she let out a sigh of relief. Larry lay half in the cockpit and half over the winch pad groaning loudly. Janet nudged him in the hip with her foot. Slowly Larry sat up, his eyes slightly glazed.

"Here are some seasick pills, better have two." Slowly Larry's eyes began to focus again. He sat up straighter, and his mouth became firmer.

"You take one first," he snarled and he pulled the pistol from his belt. "I think those chips were poisoned. I don't trust you. In fact, I want you to take four of those pills. If they really are seasick pills, they won't hurt you. Do it. Do it now!" He pointed the gun at her face and started to squeeze the trigger.

"OK. Look, I'm taking them." She popped a pill in her mouth and hid it under her tongue while pretending to swallow. "There, see. They are seasick pills." She opened her mouth and showed him her tongue.

"Take another and swallow that one and the one under your tongue. Or I will shoot your daughter as she is sleeping. Do it!" He aimed his gun down at the berth. Janet swallowed in fright, looking down at her innocent child. "Take another, now, now!" She forced another pill in between her teeth and resigned she gulped it down her throat, helped with a sip from

Larry's can of coke. "Alright, now take two more, I want to be sure they aren't poisoned."

Larry watched her carefully. Janet steered the 'Rose Marie' slightly more upwind so the boat started to corkscrew down the waves. Larry's face started to turn even greener. After a few minutes, in a rush, Larry grabbed the bottle of pills and emptied the bottle into his mouth. He washed them down with the rest of the coke and went back to holding on.

"This better work you little bitch or I am going to screw you so bad you'll never be able to walk again. And that is a promise."

Janet felt her eyes begin to close. She struggled to stay awake. She looked over at Larry. He was leaning against the winch pad again, eyes closed and greener than ever. Quietly she felt around in the cockpit locker and found a clothes peg. She threw it at her sleeping husband still down below. It missed. She thought about whispering but Larry still had his finger on the trigger of his gun. Maybe he was asleep, maybe he wasn't. She found a bag of pegs and looked over at Larry. His eyes were closed. She started throwing the clothes pegs one at a time at Harv. One of them hit him on the nose. Harv just rolled over and started snoring.

Despite herself, Janet started giggling quietly to herself. She found a small piece of rope and threw that at him. He swatted at it in his sleep like a mosquito. It didn't help that she was falling asleep.

Janet threw a deck brush that just missed his face. She started giggling again. Then she found a soaking wet sponge that landed splat on his face as she laid her head on the steering wheel and started to close her eyes.

Harv sat up, water all over his face, and looked in wonder at the wild assortments of things laying all over the berth and floor. He saw Janet in the cockpit falling asleep at the wheel.

He stumbled over to the companionway as Janet woke, put her fingers to her lips and then pointed at the apparently sleeping Larry. She put her wrists together and then motioned a circle around her wrists. Harv, now awake, nodded, ducked below and was soon back with a roll of duct tape. He studied the situation for a minute. The gun was still pointed in the general direction of Janet. He motioned for his wife to slide over to port as far as she could without leaving the wheel.

He tried to unroll the tape as quietly as he could but it made an unholy noise. Larry jerked back awake and waved the gun around.

"What is going on here? Hey, you. Keep steering the boat, woman." Janet slid back behind the wheel and pointedly avoided looking at Harv who had scurried forward. She felt her eyes start to close again.

"Keep your eyes open, girl," murmured Larry as his eyes started to close again. "Just cuz I close my eyes don't mean nothing. I'm still awake, you better believe that, little lady. You damn well better believe that."

Harv slipped into the head and then tiptoed back aft. He had three feet of duct tape unrolled and he was struggling to keep the tape straight and untwisted. It tried to fold in on itself constantly. He motioned to Janet to grab Larry's hands and hold them straight out so he could wrap the tape around Larry's hands. She shook her head no and pointed at the gun. It was still pointed at her. She didn't believe he was asleep, yet; he should be, what with all the pills he took.

The boat seemed to be answering to the auto helm at the moment so she scooted over to the port side, behind Larry's head, forward of him along the rail and whispered.

"Larry, Larry, wake up, Larry. I have your money, Larry." He didn't seem to respond. "Larry, you hunk, I'm naked." Larry still seemed dead to the world.

Janet signaled to Harv that she was going to grab the gun and throw it over the side. Harv shook his head and mouthed, 'No.' She ignored him and grabbed Larry's gun arm and banged his hand against the rail. The gun made a satisfying plop as it fell into the water. Larry slept thru the whole thing.

Quickly Harv wrapped the tape ten times around the man's wrists. Larry never woke up.

"Fantastic. Bloody fantastic!" Janet murmured and promptly fell asleep. Harv gently lay her down on the lee cockpit seat with a cushion under her pretty head, taped up Larry's ankles and changed course to the small island of Geronimo ten miles away.

XIV

Any City in the World

Peterson planned to take Janney out on the town. He wanted to show her a real good time and forget the frustrations of the office at the same time. They had planned to meet at the restaurant but at the last minute he changed his mind and drove to the marina and her boat. He had to see her and he just had to see her right now. At the head of the dock he paused with second thoughts. What if she was seeing someone else? What if he walked in on some private portion of her life? What if she was just being kind to some guy without a clue? With a curse he walked down the dock.

"If it is meant to be, it is meant to be. If it is love then I can do no wrong," he whispered to himself but his eyes reflected worry and doubt. He looked wearily at his reflection in the window of a nearby power boat.

"What the hell am I doing?" He looked at all the closed boats. Everyone had a story. He was sure Janney had a secret story, herself. Everyone did. What if she had done something illegal in her life and was on the lam?

He hadn't had much luck with women in his life. He always told himself that cops shouldn't marry anyway, but his mouth tasted of sour grapes afterwards. Other cops around him had bragged of their conquests and he had made up a few lies to be one of the boys but inside there was always a bit of sadness and a bit of fear when he looked at a beautiful woman. There were always the whores, usually free for cops but something, he didn't know what, made him shy away from them. Using his hand was cleaner and safer. But it was, oh, so lonely.

"Shit," he growled and with a violent push against a cleat he strode down the dock. He stopped outside her dock and with his policeman's knock pounded harshly on the hull.

"Who is it?" called a woman's voice.

"Peterson." He heard a wood hatch opening. Slowly the companionway doors opened. She stood there, a smile on her face, wearing a bathrobe and a towel over her wet hair.

"Hi, Lieutenant. I thought we were going to meet at the restaurant? Is everything OK? Has anything happened?"

"No, Janney. I just couldn't stand, I mean, I wanted to, what I mean to say is I was in the neighborhood. Is everything all right with you, Janney?"

"Oh, yes, silly. Well as long as you are here why don't you come in while I get ready? I'll just be a minute." She closed the doors behind him and started to rub her hair inside the towel. He looked around the small but tidy boat. A tiny kitchen led off on one side while on the other a darkened doorway led to the master bedroom.

"This is a beautiful yacht, how do you manage," he turned back towards her. She had her back to him and was leaning over her long hair almost touching the deck as she fluffed her hair with the towel. He gulped seeing the beautiful curves of her feminine form. She peeked slyly at him upside down. His mouth sagged open.

"Do you like what you see, sailor?" Slowly she stood up and turned to face him. "We don't have to go and eat right now this very second, do we?" It seemed an accident that her bathrobe had fallen open and showed a bit of cleavage. She breathed deep expanding her chest and said,

"Would you like something to drink?" His hands became sweaty and he wiped them nervously on his pant legs. He was sure it was his fault her towel had slipped. He was the one who came unannounced. He was making her uncomfortable. That was it. It was always the same. He didn't know the right things to say to a beautiful woman. They were awkward because of him.

"Yeah, sure, I could really go for a drink right now. There is no hurry to get to the restaurant. It isn't that busy on week nights, besides they know me and will hold my reservation. And, well, I, you see, I, I guess I should have met you there instead of coming here, and…"

She regally glided into the galley seemingly without moving her legs. He stared, mouth open, she seemed a princess to him. So sure of herself, so composed, her head held so high as if she really was wearing a crown. "Want a beer, lover?" she asked over a beautifully shaped shoulder. He gaped, open mouthed, speechless.

When she came back with his beer the belt on her bathrobe had somehow become loosened. He felt his nervousness increase, somehow reinforced in her presence.

"Why don't you get comfortable? Is it hot in here or is it just me?" She tugged at her robe and he could almost see the nipples of her breasts now. She sat on the settee with her back as straight as a board and raised one leg, heel on the table. Her foot was beautiful. So slim, so elegant. Her toes were painted a brilliant red. Her bathrobe accidently fell open around her knee and sank half way to her hips.

He gulped again. She looked like a Hollywood starlet. She was so composed and sure of herself. So much of everything he was not. What could she see in him? If she only knew that he wanted to make love to her, right then and now, why, she would think him the most terrible man alive.

"Why don't you come over here and sit next to me, I won't bite but I may nibble," she smiled. Peterson walked over to the settee on unsteady legs. He sat down on the other end and nervously crossed his arms. He held his body rigid, like a soldier saluting.

"I wonder if you could aid a citizen in distress, Lieutenant?" she asked. "I seem to have something in my eye. It is really bothering me. It is very painful. Could you take a look?" Without waiting for an answer she slithered over on the cushion and laid her head on Peterson's lap.

"It is the right eye. Can you see anything? It may be very little. Please, could you look very closely?"

Peterson stared into her eyes. They were beautifully shaped, very clear, with long lashes. A perfume seemed to seep out of her skin and its scent enveloped him. He stared deep into her eyes for a few minutes.

"I don't see anything in either eye, Janney." He put his hand on her forehead and petted her hair. She had hair like a cat, velvety and smooth. It was a pleasure to stroke it.

"That feels so good when you stroke my hair. Your hands are so strong and so masculine. Tell me what you are thinking right now. Don't make up something. You have to tell the truth. Close your eyes and tell me what you are thinking right now at this very second."

"I, I can't believe how comfortable you are in your own skin. I have always been so shy about, about, well about my desires and feelings. I find it very difficult to share myself with others."

"Oh, me, too. Don't be fooled by how I am now. I have always been shy. Just recently I had an experience, it was terrible in a way, it destroyed the person I was I think, the shy introverted person, but it allowed out a new me, a me I never knew existed. I never knew I could feel so much, I never knew I could respond like they talk about in the magazines at the grocery counter, I always thought I was a bit of a cold fish, you know? I even thought for a while I was frigid.

"I hated it at first. I hated what he did to me. He hurt me so much, he used me like a toy; he never asked if he could, he just did everything he wanted. I tried to struggle as much as I could, he was very, very strong, but it didn't matter what I did. He broke me, he broke the mold, the pattern, the essence of what was me. He changed how I thought of myself; he changed how I felt about my person, about my womanhood.

"But now, it is like I have this new body with incredible, super powers I never knew I had, and you are the first person to meet the new me, and, well, try me out. Don't take this the wrong way, but I feel like I am almost a virgin, but a naughty experienced virgin. It is OK to be shy like I used to be. Just go with the flow. You are the most handsome man I have met since I became the new me." And then she thought, 'Or, second most handsome.'

She reached up and loosened his tie. Then slowly began to unbutton his shirt. He opened her robe and dropped it off her shoulders as he kissed her softly in the hollow of her neck. He let her robe lay as it fell on the sofa in a gentle pile.

She pulled his shirt up pinning his arms and then raised her head and sucked his nipples. She felt them harden between her lips and she began nibbling on them. With each increasingly stronger nip he felt himself harden between his legs until he was certain he was bigger than he had ever been in his life. He struggled out of his shirt and cupped her breasts. She guided his left hand to her right breast, his right hand till he was over her lower unclothed belly.

"Kiss my neck, lover. Suck my neck. Oh, go ahead, bite my throat." He lowered his right hand down between her legs but she pulled it back up to her belly. She arranged his hand, thumb in the navel, fingers down. As he nibbled at her throat, her back arched beneath him and she threw her head back, putting herself at his mercy. "Take me. Enjoy me. I am yours. Use me. Hurt me. Fuck me."

He felt himself engorge to unbelievable size. He couldn't stand it anymore. It was just too much. He stood up with her in his arms; he lifted her up into the air in one motion, it was as if she weighed nothing. He held her high in the air and slowly lowered her onto his manhood. As her face came level with his, as he was inserted fully into her, as he felt her insides pulsing, vibrating, their lips met, joined, welded together, and rational thought was lost to both of them.

Later he found himself somehow in her bed with her curled in his arms, snoring softly. He petted her head with his free hand and gazed at this unbelievable creature. It was like she was a force of nature. So elemental, so wild, so natural, so right. He started to feel the first chink fall in the wall he had built around himself in almost twenty years on the force.

'Maybe there is more, more than just right and wrong," he thought, lying beside her. 'Maybe sometimes it is the good and beautiful against the weak and cowardly; the whole being instead the broken half person.' And he fell back asleep with a smile on his face and her breast in his hand.

XV

Any Jail in the United States

Lucy woke up with water running down her face. She shook her head and looked up. Ann Roberts was casually shooting her in the face with a water pistol. She shook her head again and then remembered what had occurred before. Her eyes widened and she stared, aghast, at Ann Roberts.

"You aren't going to let that monster hurt me, kill me, or," she gulped, "eat me, are you?" Her eyes were begging, her mouth twisted in horror. Her manacled hands tried to come forward to plea and beg.

"You haven't answered my questions, fully and honestly. Personally, I can't see how I can prevent you from being returned to that cell. It is the cell assigned to you. This jail suffers from over crowding. We can't legally give you a different cell. It would mean putting a more honest, more cooperative inmate in your old cell, in Joy's cell. Now if you don't have anything else to add to your statement, I am a busy woman." She started fussing with her pens and pads.

"No, please. Anything. Ask me, anything. I'll talk. But promise me, please promise me, you won't put me back in that cell. Please." Tears were running down her cheeks. She felt wetness between her legs. She realized, in embarrassment and in horror, that she had wet herself in terror. "I'll talk, I'll talk. Please, please let me talk."

"What other crimes have you committed? Don't omit anything. This is your last chance. Don't blow it. You know what will happen if you do. Talk." Ann Roberts looked at her as if made of stone, unfeeling, uncaring, cold, hard, lifeless granite.

And Lucy talked. She told every thing she knew or guessed. She talked and talked and talked till any self respect she had was torn out of her soul with her words.

She talked and as she talked she shrank within herself. She started as a beautiful young woman and three hours later ended her questioning as a haggard, beaten, dull, lifeless crone. Afterwards, it didn't matter if she returned to Joy's cell or not, there wasn't anything left inside of her to be killed. She was the living dead. The woman who stood tall and defiant on the counter of the grocery store was long gone. The woman who could stop any car on the highway with her beautiful spirit and flashing eyes was dead. Lucy no longer lived. What was left was a beaten, lifeless, old woman in a 24 year old body; a body to soon degenerate with disuse and lack of care. The body that once had been Lucy would be dead within a year. The Law and Justice had triumphed again.

XVI

Off the Baja Coast

They anchored off a sandy beach on the south coast of the small island of Geronimo. No other boats were there. At times there was a lobster fishing camp on the island. At the moment it was vacant. It was a lonely island far from the mainland of Baja California. The most dominant sound at the moment was the endless crashing surf along the northern coast and a young girl yelling.

"Alright, Mom! Way to go, Mom! Mom, wake up, Mom! Dad! I can't wake up Mom!"

"Go back to sleep, Jill. Your mom took some anti-depressants. Go to sleep."

"Sleep? Go to sleep? Never again! Why did Mom take pills? Who tied up Larry? Why are we anchored? Where are we? What are we going to do with Larry? Why does everything exciting take place when I am asleep? Dad, wake up! I'm trying to talk to you! Can I punch the pirate on the nose? Dad!"

Slowly Harv stumbled to the stove, lit it and managed to start the coffee. He turned his blurry eyes towards Larry who still seemed dead to the world. Janet was stirring. She held her hands over her eyes as if she had the world's biggest headache. Harv handed her a cup of coffee loaded with sugar and milk. Slowly she pulled herself into a sitting position and sipped herself back into a lower level of consciousness.

"Mom, I can't believe you took drugs. You always tell me 'just say no'. Mom, I am very disappointed in you. Where is your self respect? If you don't respect yourself, how can you expect others to respect you? Now, that I have lectured you, how did you tie up the dirty pirate?"

"Baby, can't you just go back to bed? I have a terrible headache."

"Mom! Come on! I am never going to sleep again! All the exciting stuff happens after I fall asleep."

"Larry was feeling seasick so I told him to eat a bunch of greasy, acidic food. He got seasick. I gave him Valium which he believed was Dramamine, he fell asleep, your Dad tied him up. There, now go to bed." She looked vaguely in the direction of her husband, her eyes having trouble focusing. "Harv, what are we going to do with him?"

"Throw him to the sharks, keel haul him, string him up the yardarm, skin him alive, throw mud balls all over him, maroon him like Robinson Crusoe, I'll fart right in his face!"

"Jill! Really, Jill. Honey, if we do something bad to him, we become no better than he is. We can't murder him. He is a human being, after all. We do owe him something, he did save you from that guy in the showers. We can't kill him. I wouldn't feel right leaving him ashore. He might die. What do you think, Harv?"

"Let me see if our handheld radio will reach anyone. We can call for the police. Where is that valise he was always carrying around?"

"I'll get it Dad!" She raced down into the cabin. Janet massaged her temples. Jill was soon back with the valise. "You guys aren't going to believe this but we are rich!" She yanked open the bag and showed her parents. The bag was filled, almost to the top, with money. Harv lifted the handheld off the top. He turned it on.

"Pan pan, pan pan, pan pan," he called. Only static replied. "This is the American sailing vessel, 'Rosie Marie' with a non life threatening emergency on board. Can anyone hear me?" Again all he heard was static. "We might be too far out to sea for anyone to hear us. Janet, you try. Sometimes a woman's voice can cut through the static. Jill, time to put all that book learning to work. We better count all this money so we can tell the authorities how much it is."

"We are going to give it back? Dad! He ruined our trip. He is a bad, bad pirate. It is our money now, for sure. Its our booty, Dad! Our pirate booty!"

"Count it, Jill, and no cheating. We aren't crooks. And neither are you. Right?"

"OK, yeah, right. I guess. But," Her father gave her a stern look. "OK, Dad. Can I just keep a little, Sir Daddy? Just a little as a finder's fee? Can I, Wonderful Sir Daddy?"

"That isn't up to us. But it is up to us to be true to ourselves. We aren't living on the dark side, are we, Luke Waterwalker."

"Oh, Dad, that movie is so over-the-hill." Slowly she started sorting the bills into different piles between mumbles about yardarms, black spots and deserted isles...

XVII

In the Badlands of Mexico

Raoul was born to deceit and lying and violence in the warrens of Mexico City. His mother had turned him into a beggar two days after he was born. She shoved him in people's faces and asked for money. When he was young and small she made a good living. To keep him little she fed him as little as she could. Little was good. Sick was good. Somehow, only the Aztec gods knew how, he survived till he was seven. At that age his begging value was almost zero. His mother considered cutting his legs off or poking both eyes out to increase her earnings. As practice, she would push her thumbs into the corners of his eyes to test how difficult it would be to gouge them out. She would pretend her hand was a machete and saw at his legs to build up her nerve. He was only saved when she was talked into selling him to a compatriot who wanted to use his small size in a burglary team.

He was so small he could fit through the iron rungs that protected every window in the city. Once inside he had to open a door that was huge to him. It was all he could do to even reach the door handle. And as far as the latches securing the tops of the doors, they were way out of reach. He was beaten badly for each failure. That isn't what scared him most. His greatest fear was being stepped on by the huge feet of the owner's of the houses when they discovered him. Eventually he learned to use furniture to reach the doors and carried a stick with a hook tied to it to help with the door latches. He tried so hard to please everyone, just as he had tried to please his mother. It didn't help. He wasn't rewarded when he did everything right; he just wasn't beaten. He was given just enough food to keep him alive. Everyone wanted to keep him little.

He learned to steal at the market just to get something to eat. With practice, he improved his skills. He tried pocketing jewelry during burglaries. To punish him, the gang members, who were ready for him to rebel, dislocated both arms at the shoulders. This, they said, made it easier for him to fit between the bars. At night they fit two boards to the sides of his head and lashed them tightly together to make his head narrower. Despite the torture and lack of food, he became stronger. On what he thought might be his 10th birthday, he escaped. He had no idea how old he really was. Five year old kids were bigger than he was. He counted back, with what little math he had, and decided he was ten. Time to leave, before they decided he was too big and crushed his chest.

He took up with a gang of children. Children was the wrong name. They were evil, cruel assassins. He killed his first man at eleven, his first woman at twelve. But he did finally eat well, if he could. The gang members fought for the best of the food. He learned to use his fists and his unnaturally long arms; his shoulders had never recovered from being dislocated.

He was born with a small penis. Even fully enlarged it barely reached two inches. He had to fight to prove his manliness. How he cursed his parents for creating him. How he cursed his mother for forming him. How he cursed society for being bigger, stronger, more endowed, and against him. He became accomplished with knifes and guns. He was forced by the gang to kill men, women, and children. After his tenth kill, he started to like it.

It was a woman. She looked so much like his mother. Her husband paid a good price to get her to disappear from the face of the earth, without a trace. If Raoul had been a kinder man he would have given the money back. After he dislocated her arms and gouged out her eyes, he took his time killing her, cutting off piece after piece, feeding it to the hogs. Finally, when there was little human about her, he threw the still alive torso into the pen where the hungry hogs tore open her body to feast on the guts before eating the bones, skull, sinews, muscles.

It would have destroyed a lesser man; the horror of it. The sounds of the hogs feasting amidst her fainter and fainter cries. The sight of two hogs fighting over her heart; tearing it apart in the end; snorting, grunting, shoving, eating. The horror of it. The pigs eating her intestines like spaghetti. The bloody horror. The getting back at his mother, but not his mother, loving the kill, loving the crying agony, hating the over whelming fact that he still loved his stupid, idiotic, cruel, inhumane mother.

How he had envied larger men when he was younger. Not now. No way, now. So many of them had felt the steel of his knife and the lead of his gun that he no longer had respect for size. No one expected a man as small as he to fight back. By fourteen, he had a record with the police and they were actively seeking him. By sixteen, he was in jail for life.

In prison he discovered a talent for terror. Prison was fine if one was tall and strong. If not, and he wasn't, it was playtoy time. At least it was until he bit off and ate his first cock. How the man beat on him as he bit, how the man cried as he swallowed. When they started to wait for him in dark corners, when they planed to torture and kill him, he started his first gang. He enlisted one con at a time. He let his members use his little ass as a reward. With the big, the strong, and the vicious surrounding him, he felt he was safe.

It was a good thing he was small. He was spared working at the old hydraulic machines inmates were required to operate that were so dangerous they took a man's hand or arm each month. They assigned him to help with the library as he lied and told them he could read and write. Between the stacks of books, he found men would pay to use his little body. And pay well. Extra well as they thought he was educated. His gang grew until he was a force in the pen. A force to be reckoned with. When the escape attempt came they took him along, as a man thin enough to go thru small windows can be very useful; and he was a diversion to use during the inevitable waiting during the escape.

He was second out of the tunnel and kicked one of the supports holding up the roof as he was almost out. The men behind him wouldn't be using him any longer. The one in front? He cut his Achilles tendon with a sharp piece of glass as he crawled away. The screws were so busy digging out bodies and capturing the screaming cripple, that he got away, clean.

He went up into the hills and then the mountains. He preyed upon isolated farms. He liked it when the man was away and he could do what he wanted to the wife. He liked to tie them up and slowly cut off their arms first with rusty tools. Then he gouged out their eyes with a screwdriver. Any children he killed first without thought. There were too many children in the world. He was sure the planet was thanking him whenever he killed more of them. Soon he was armed, well fed, and had found the beginnings of a new gang. Some called him a revolutionary. They called him a terrorist. They called him a hero. He just laughed at them. Laughed and then killed them. He killed any who stood up. Any who stood taller than he. Any

one with beauty. Any who judged. Any who thought. Any.
Any. All.

With in a year he was the most wanted man in Mexico.
Fame made him just more violent, more cruel, and far more
predatory. His gang numbered over fifty, each more cruel and
lethal than anyone in the Mexican Policia.

They sent the army out after him with helicopters,
mortars, snipers and dogs. He laughed at their inept attempts.
It wasn't till the President of the United States of Mexico asked
the President of the United States of America for help with their
spy satellites that he felt pressure. The satellites could see the
tracks his trucks made, even when he hid his gang in caves.

They sent helicopters after him and soon his gang was
dwindling, some were killed, most simply drifted away. They
almost caught him twice in box canyons and finally, in
desperation, he caught a ferry boat in the middle of the night
and went to Baja California. There was little law in Baja, no
helicopters, and no army in such a forsaken place. The small
hills they called mountains held few farms, the deserts they
called plains were uninhabited except for crazed gringos racing
through them on motorcycles and dune buggies, the coasts
held few cities and in them the inhabitants were so hardened
by their fierce clime that they had little fear of him and his
gang. The only ones that feared him were the many gringos in
motor homes and yachts.

He liked to prey on the yachts. They always had liquor on
the boat and good things to eat. Their bodies were so soft.
Most of them had lived their lives in air-conditioned offices and
homes in El Norte and had come down to Mexico to try to see
what the world was like. He showed them. Jesus, did he ever
show them. If they wanted to find
out what Mexico was like, they found out. After he tired of the
women, he cut a hole in the men's belly button and fucked
them in the stomach after he tied them down, stretched over a
log. He liked their moans and cries as he forced himself over
and over again into their bellies. His little penis finally found a
tight enough hole to excite him. Each thrust into their bellies
was a spear, each explosion, full of the many diseases he
carried. Afterwards, after a day of repeated lust, he laughed as
their abdomens swelled with infection and their guts erupted in
geyser-like bursts out of the slit in their belly buttons.

His gang wasn't much better. They followed him, in
return he fed them horror in large doses. They seemed to need

permission to be bad. They seemed somehow to be allowed to torture and kill and rape. He wasn't shy. He welded them to him with not only permission but encouragement.

There were few policia in Baja. And this time the army didn't come. Mexico City didn't care what happened in far away Baja. They didn't care what happened to people on yachts and motor homes. They only cared about the tourists in hotels. He killed, he maimed, he destroyed, he gloried in his evilness.

And each time, the infections in his body growing, swelling in his brain, he became worse, more terrible, beyond cruel, beyond insane, beyond belief. And glorying in it.

XVIII

The Port of San Diego

Life was different for Peterson. He laughed more, he looked forward to getting up in the morning, and he let Maria run the Department her way or any way she wanted. He didn't care. It seemed inane to him to care. If downtown didn't care, why should he? This was a free ride, wasn't it? A bonus, a pre-retirement job, a reward for a career of hard work.

He showed up in the mornings and signed whatever Maria asked him to sign. He let Maria decide which crimes to investigate, which men to assign where, he sat in his office and waited impatiently till it was lunch time and he could meet Janney. He always went early. He stopped at little shops to buy her a trinket. He never looked at the price tag. He had been well paid for eighteen years and never before had anyone to spoil. He never had anyone special before. He had the department use direct deposit all those years; they placed his wages in the bank like clockwork. He needed very little to survive; survival was all he was interested in then. Why spend money on an apartment he only slept in? And then rarely? Now, it was different. Now, he had a life outside the department. Now, he found a girl that loved him. Finally. He had finally found someone who loved him, not his money, not his ability to appropriate whatever drugs they might want, not for his high performance undercover car, just him. She loved just him. Just little old dopey him. He cried at the thought.

His life was the best it had ever been. Every night he took Janney out on the town. Every night they ended up at his place or her boat. Life was good. Except every night as they fell asleep, Janney asked him if he had any news about the sailboat with the family, the one with the rapist on board, the 'Rose Marie'. Every night he lied and said he was working on it.

One night he tired of lying. Tired of lying to the one he loved more and more each day. The next morning he got to work early, he was the first one there. He caught up on all the faxes they had received about the boat. Ensenada, Cabo San Lucas, La Paz, Mazatlan and Puerto Vallarta, none of the Mexican clearance ports had heard from any boat called the 'Rose Marie'. It was as if they had dropped off the face of the earth.

When Maria came in he started his new plan. It was called, 'Find the 'Rose Marie', so Janney would 'Really Fall in Love with Him.' He wanted that woman, he wanted to spend the rest of his life with her, he didn't care where in the world they were as long as he could wake up with her wonderful smoky grey eyes gazing at him in the early morning light. He didn't care how they lived as long as her wonderful lovemaking made him feel he was eighteen again. He didn't care if the world went to hell as long as he and Janney were in heaven. The steel blue walls that had formed a career police officer's personality were falling off all around him; and he didn't care.

"Maria, we have to find that boat, the 'Rose Marie'. What haven't we done? There must be some other avenue we haven't explored. What is it, Maria, come on, think."

"Captainne, there are many things we can do, but we don't have the men or the dollars. We have done all that is expected of us." Maria stopped and thought for a minute. "There are two things we can do.

"I have talked to Jose. He can fly you down the coast anytime this week. The tuna boat, she is in the dry dock, so he has the time."

Then in a rush she said, "Captainne, there is one more thing we can try. We can get the SSB radio to be here in the office. There are many peoples talking on the radio every morning on sailboats and fishing boats. They talk all the time, about everything. But we can't talk to them. We don't have this thing, this SSB radio. We should buy one and put it here in the office, there is room, right here on my desk. That way I can tell you when there in news of them. What do you think, Captainne?" He sat down on the edge of her desk and thought for a minute.

"It could work, Maria, it could work. How much do these radios cost?"

"Captainne, I will find out and make the purchase order. Tomorrow you can sign it. Then we can find this boat. That is good news, no?" Peterson nodded and returned to his desk, shuffling paperwork, waiting for lunch.

'This is very good. Captainne will be happy and I will be able to talk to Manuel every night when he is off on the fishing boat.' She hugged herself in delight as she thought, 'Life was so good when one is in love.'

XIX

Isla Geronimo, Mexico

Larry Adams had trained himself for years to wake up without moving a muscle. He listened, smelled, and felt for every clue he could acquire before opening his eyes every morning for years. So, it was no different now as he regained conscienceless. He could smell someone cooking and hear the clatter of dishes and a woman singing to his left and down below him. That would mean he was still in the cockpit on the left side. Port side, he thought they called it. His hands were tied some how. He couldn't tell till he moved his hands, and that would give away the fact that he was awake if anyone was watching. He felt hard wood beneath him and the sun shining on him. That also would indicate he was in the cockpit and it was daylight. To his right he heard a girl complaining to herself about school work; that would be Jill, the girl. But where was the man? After five minutes of listening, he chanced a peak, just a brief crack of his eyelids. He saw his hands wrapped with duct tape and a large mass directly in front of him. He quickly closed him eyes again; and laughed to himself at the stupidity of these sailors. Think of all the rope on this boat, and they tied him up with duct tape! Duct tape! Great stuff if you wanted to seal an air conditioning duct. Not so great to tie up a man in the know. God, you would think they would know. A guy can rip it in half with just his finger tips. Isn't it obvious?

Just then he heard the faintest sound, just a hint of cloth on wood and then there was a hand on his throat.

"I saw your eyes open, Larry. I know you are awake. We have you tied up hand and foot with duct tape. You can't escape. We were just talking about what to do with you. We can leave you on this island, no one is here now but sooner or later some fishermen will come. I think this is the best choice. We can throw you over board with chains around your feet. No one likes that solution. Or we can keep you secured, tied up till we reach the police, maybe in Turtle Bay. Then they can do what they want with you. Do you see any other solution?"

With a sudden twist of his wrists, one wrist down, one up, Larry ripped the duct tape in half, ripping it across the bias, sideways. Pushing himself, launching himself off the seat with his now free hands he knocked the hand off his throat and lunged at Harv, pushed him towards the side of the boat till he hit his lower legs, just below the knees against the life line. Harv wind milled his arms, trying to regain his balance. Just when he thought he might be OK, Larry gave just a little push with a finger and over he went.

As Harv fell over the rail, Larry felt movement to his left and saw a flash of silver from the corner of his eye. The woman! A knife! He turned right and dove down the companionway hatch leading to the stern cabin and landed on a bed full of money and girl. Janet scrambled over to the cabin companionway and swung her knife again, at Larry's back, just missing. She saw him fall down the stern hatch, his bulk filling the hatch, and she threw her knife straight at him, straight at the middle of his back, straight at his heart, then as he landed and then he turned away exposing Jill, sitting on the berth. He continued his roll and Janet watched in horror as the spinning knife landed and plunged deep into Jill's left breast, her hands full of the money she had been counting.

Jill's eyes opened wide in surprise. Janet saw her lips form the word 'Mommy'. She saw her eyes glaze over, one little hand touch the blade and then she fell back onto the berth and was still.

Harv reappeared, soaking wet as Janet started screaming.

"No, no, no, NO!" and she fell onto the cockpit floor, hands over her eyes, fingers intertwined in her long hair pulling, yanking, screaming, crying. Her face turned pale, almost blue.

Harv look down into the stern cabin and saw the big knife deep in his daughter's breast. So deep it must have reached her heart. Larry pulled the knife out of Jill with a jerk. He twisted Jill's inert body over his knee, belly up and looked at Harv right in the eye.

"Do you want to see your daughter's insides?" He poised the knife above Jill, the point next to her womanhood. "Do you want to see what is left of your child opened up in front of you, huh, big man, huh?"

Harv fell to his knees and threw up into the cockpit. He felt his hands being twisted behind him and tied together. He didn't fight. He just saw the big knife stuck into his daughter and heard the sucking noise as Larry pulled the knife out. His world, all that he had sworn to protect, all that he held most dear, was gone. He had failed. He had failed his sacred trust. His reason to be. His reason to live, was fading. His breath came shallower and shallower. His chest felt tight and his left arm started to hurt.

Larry finished tying Harv up and started with Janet. As he tied her hands in front of her, she suddenly seemed to come out of her shock.

"No, No. Harv. Stop it. Don't let it happen. No, No, No." Harv came out of his decline. His wife was calling. He still had a duty to perform. They, someone, somewhere, still needed him. He sat up, struggling against his bonds. He was next to Janet. Her hands were tied to her feet, arms on either side of her knees. She was propped up head and knees down, her behind was up in the air. Her eyes were opened but unfocused. Larry sat across from them, tapping the knife against his palm. There wasn't any blood on the blade. Larry must have wiped it off on his daughter's hair or clothes or skin. Such a bastard. Using his daughter like a rag. He deserved to die.

"Things are different now, aren't they? You two are going to do exactly as I say or I will cut up your daughter's body, piece by piece and feed it to the sharks, and you two will watch every action. And Harv, if you even think of doing something stupid..." He reached over and ran the knife between Janet's skin and shorts and cut her shorts off her.

"Don't even think of doing something stupid. I guarantee, you will never be able to live with yourself, if you do, Harv. You still have your woman. She will need you. But I promise you. I will hurt her so bad, and I'll make you watch, make you watch things that will destroy your mind. You will go insane. So Don't! DON'T DO ANYTHING STUPID!"

XX

Aloft over the Pacific Ocean

Peterson sat next to Jose, Maria's friend, in the copilot's seat. It wasn't a big chopper but it seemed to be working so far. Every non-essential piece of equipment had been removed to prolong time aloft. Every piece of metal had been replaced with fiberglass except for the blades. Even the doors were missing. The helicopter's only reason to exist was to find fish for its mother ship. The longer it could stay aloft, the more fish they could catch. They had taken off from the ship in the harbor in the dry dock and headed directly south. Peterson had asked if they had to clear customs to go into Mexico.

"Oh, Senor, the Aduna, they are too much trouble. We stay low, OK? We go under the radar. The 'Aquila' here, there is little metal in her. They cannot see us. The Aduna, the Customs, they take hours; then they always want the mordita, the, how you say, the bribe. We will be back in the El Norte before they are out of the bed!"

It seemed to be the truth. No jet fighters buzzed them and the radio was silent. No one was interested in them. The helicopter rumbled past Ensenada.   A few sailboats were in the harbor, a few more were out in the Todos Santos Islands.

None of them were the 'Rose Marie'. He could see white caps out to the west, farther out, and a lot of kelp along the coast. The copter droned on heading south.

"Look, Senor, down there. That is Cabo Colnett. You see the valley running down the middle of the cliff? Right there, see? When I was a boy, my father, he took me fishing and we caught so many langosta that the boat, she was sinking. You could not believe it. Everywhere on the boat there were the langosta. We stood on them. We sat on them. My father and I, we bailed the boat all night long. Then in the morning we caught some more! It is the truth, Senor! With the monies, my father, he bought me a red bicycle. I had the first bicycle in my village."

Peterson just nodded. He watched the water as they headed south. So far they had seen ten boats, eight sailboats and two power vessels. None were the 'Rose Marie'. The sea seemed so endless. It was easy to believe that a boat could just disappear in such an ocean.

"Senor, look. That is San Quentin. It has a beautiful beach, see? Look. A beach like that, it makes all the beaches in Norte California look little, si? And, there, to the right; that island? Si, that is the Isla San Martin. That island is the limit we can go today. We go around it to look, OK? Then we have to go back for the gasolina. It's a nice island, si? Long ago, the bad man, the pirate, Francis Drake, he hide there and then attacked the noble Spanish ships for their gold. My brother and I, when we were young, one day we took my father's boat and we went there. We dug many holes but we could not find any treasure. The pirates, they hid it too well."

The island looked like a poor hiding place to Peterson. It was fairly round with a tall volcanic cone in the middle. He guessed the pirates must have put a lookout on top of the mountain. There was no sign of habitation and no boats.

"There, Senor, see? Far away to the south? That is the Isla Geronimo. It is named for your famous Indian, as are the reefs to the south. No, today we cannot see the reefs; they say the reefs jump out of the water like Geronimo and grab any passing boat. Mucho peligrosa, Senor. Very dangerous."

The chopper started its long flight back to San Diego. Jose was quiet and Peterson thought about his life as a police officer. He had many memories too, but most were memories of death, and blood; of terror and boredom. He remembered the time he had raced to the hospital with a woman about to give birth in the back of his cruiser. He had sped through red lights and turned corners on two wheels. It was a wonder he hadn't killed them both, killed all three. Later he had learned that the hospital had sent the mother to another facility as she didn't have the right insurance and that she had died on the operating table at a fly by night emergency room. He didn't know what happened to the child, or even if it had lived. He had many memories he tried his best to forget. He was a man without a past. Or one who tried as hard as he could not to remember his past.

He searched his memory but he couldn't remember having an experience like Jose's. Of bailing all night long with a boat full of lobsters or looking for Sir Francis Drake's famed treasure.

He wondered if it was too late for him. Was he doomed to remember nothing but the horror of his life on the day he died? Of risks taken for nothing? To wake in the morning and remember only the nightmare of the night. The nightmare of death, of securing a prisoner only to have another perp attack him from behind. After a while, the nightmares became his life, he couldn't distinguish between his real life and his dreams. His horror dreams became his life, his life became a nightmare. At night he woke from his dreams soaked in sweat. He woke to discover his throat and teeth raw from yelling and clenching. Terror became his life, sadness his only daytime emotion.

Was it too late for him to build a new life? Was this what it was all about? You live and you die? Or like him, you exist and you die? Surely his life could mean something. Something he could remember with pride on the day he died. Something he could share with loved ones. To even have loved ones. To have something or someone special. To be able to smile with happy memories at the moment of death.

Janney was his last chance. She was such a great girl. He loved her so much. He had to find this stupid boat, Janney wanted it found, so he wanted to find it. If he could find it, maybe it could cement his relationship with her. He realized that she was using him to find the boat. He didn't care. He wanted her in his life no matter how he got her there. She might be using him, but he was using her, too. She was giving him a life, a love, a reason to live. A way to smile in his sleep rather than scowl. He had to find her stupid boat for her.

Her attacker? He wasn't sure if he was even convictable. It would be hard to prove she resisted. He didn't care. Even if he did find him, chances were it would cost a fortune to get Mexico to give him up. If they thought the Americans wanted him, they would hold out for top dollar. And he doubted, downtown would foot the bill without an open and shut case. There was some thought that he was involved in a robbery at a supermarket that resulted in a death. But proving it? Downtown said they had an accomplice that could identify him. Yeah, right. He knew their ways. If they wanted a fall guy, they could get anyone to confess. He had heard all the stories. The things they did in small windowless rooms.

He had to find Janney's boat. This 'Rose Marie". His future depended on it. This might be his last chance for love. He just had to find the stupid boat. But where the hell was it?

XXI

Puebla of Turtle Bay

Raoul walked into the village of Turtle Bay, halfway down the Baja coast, halfway between San Diego and the fabulous resort of Cabo San Lucas, like a king returning to his throne. He had all that was left of his gang with him, three members. Hardened by a criminal life, they were very bad people. They truly enjoyed the hurting, the taking, the killing and the raping.

They would follow him anywhere. He fed them a diet of horror, of lust served on a platter, of destruction, of revenge against an uncomprehending world. They obeyed his every word, because he told them, he allowed them, he encouraged them to get back at the world that had ignored and hated and feared them.

The first man he saw in town was running down the street towards him; he waited till he was thirty feet away to shoot him right between the eyes. The body did a back flip and landed face down on the dusty street. The body vibrated for a few seconds, feet drumming on the ground, refusing to believe it was dead, then it was still.

He nodded to himself. His gang nodded too. Raoul's eye was in today. This town was in serious trouble. The sound of the shot brought other people out of their adobe walled, galvanized iron roofed, wood heated homes. A big man huffed towards him, full of his own importance.   He had cop written all over him.   Raoul let him get within twenty feet, then when he started shouting his pig words and Raoul shot him once between the eyes and once in the heart. He looked at the rest of the crowd with a sneer on his face. He raised his gun again. The crowd instantly disappeared.

The first store he came to was locked. It was just a little mom and pop business. He motioned to Gomez, a big burly misfit with one eye and a scar that ran halfway around his neck. He pointed to the store. Gomez hit the flimsy door with one huge fist and it fell inwards with a cloud of white dust. Raoul casually walked in and strutted over to the ice cream freezer and peered inside. An older woman crouched behind a counter on the other side shivering in fear.   He looked at Gomez.

"She is yours, amigo. Enjoy." He grabbed two sticks of ice cream, one for each hand and walked out the door as Gomez tore the clothes off the woman with ripping jerks. He jerked so hard some of her skin was torn off too. When she was naked, her yelling for help turned into screaming. Horrible, agony filled screaming.

Outside, all was quiet. Raoul walked down the street staying to one side, in the dusty shade, looking for entertainment. He found it down at the harbor. A long pier went out from the shore. Towards the end sat a sailboat. It had its anchor set and stern lines attached to the pier. He walked out on the dock and without turning his head, spoke.

"Enrique." A small squirrelly looking man ran up to Raoul and half knelt in front of him. "Liquor." He pointed at the boat and pulled a small Saturday night special revolver from his back pocket and handed it to Enrique.

With a flash Enrique ran down the stern line, was on the boat, and into the cabin. A single shot rang out and in seconds Enrique was back with a bottle of Scotch and one of Tequila. Raoul took the bottles and then nodded at the boat and told

Enrique,

"Bueno. Good work. Yours. Take anything you want." Enrique ran back and went down the hatch. Another shot was heard and then a woman's scream which went on and on until something was shoved down her throat.

Raoul walked around the small town sipping first from one bottle and then the other. He stopped in front of a small cantina. He liked the look of it. Someone had gone to a lot of work to fix it up. The paint was fresh and little decorations were here and there, signs of a woman's touch. He sat down in the shade and spoke over his shoulder.

"Simone." A woman with buzzed a haircut and a badly healed broken nose rushed up and knelt in front of him.

"Yes, Jefe," she said with a bowed head.

"Food." With a jerk she was on her feet and chopped at the locked door with her machete so fast the blade was a blur. A few shouts were heard. Within a few minutes a half naked man came out of the ruined door carrying tortillas and carne asada. Behind him came Simone. She held a rope in her hands that led between the man's legs and was attached to something there. In her other hand was her machete which was rammed into the small of the man's back.

"Bueno, Simone, take him. He is yours. Good work." With a mighty jerk Simone pulled on her rope. The man fell on the ground in agony. Simone stabbed at the man with her machete and slowly he crawled back into the building to an unthinkable fate. Raoul smiled. He was enjoying himself. He liked to play a god, dispensing fate to persons he didn't know. It made him feel like a giant. He didn't know why his gang needed permission to be evil. He just knew they did. So it might as well be him in charge.

As he sat eating his food, a woman came around the corner carrying a basket of vegetables. She was a lovely beauty, young and full of promise. She looked happy. Raoul smiled again. It was not a nice smile. By tonight she wouldn't be happy, wouldn't be beautiful, wouldn't have any hope, she might not even be alive. Raoul liked tearing down those better than he. He liked to pull the wings off flies when he was younger. He liked to pull the souls out of people now that he was older. Pull them out, sneer at them, spit at them, and grind all that they once were into the dust at his feet.

He looked at her. She had lovely brown eyes. He teased himself with the thought that he would let her go. Before she could run away, he grabbed her, forced her face down on the table and laughed at the anguish and horror on her face as he sliced her cheek from ear to mouth. As she ran away, holding her ruined face, he giggled to himself as he finished his meal and went back to drinking..

XXII

Any City, Any Where

James, did you ever find out anything about that boat, the 'Rose Marie'?" Peterson and Janney were lying in bed. They had just finished making love. Janney felt like she was glowing. She was so content. Life was so good. The only black mark was that Volcano jerk that had taken her. She didn't think she would ever get over it. He had used her so badly. But the worse part was he didn't even ask her. Somehow he had turned her into a robot. Somehow he had taken her will away from her. He had changed her into something else. He didn't care what. He just did what he wanted, without thought for others.

But now she blamed herself. Maybe there was something wrong with her. Some lack that let him take over her body and mind. She shook her head. No, she was fine. He was just a terrible, bad man. He should be killed. Executed. And she knew who could do it.

But on the other hand he had opened up something inside of her that allowed her to become a fully functioning sexual being. She didn't think her James would be interested in her if she wasn't such a wildcat in bed. Before she was such a prude, she couldn't keep a man past the first time she put out. Not now, James couldn't get enough of her. She wondered if he saw her as just an easy lay.

'Men are so stupid,' she thought. 'Women are so talented in everything they do. But men don't see that.' For a moment she felt herself start to become angry at James Peterson. Just another man, taking what he wants. Just like that Volcano. Just like all men. She felt her lips narrow and draw back in anger, she felt her eyes narrow and her nostrils flare. She rolled over to start an argument with him only to be met by his adoring eyes gazing at her.

"You are the most incredible creature on this planet, Janney. So beautiful, so smart, so very, very sexy. I love you." For a moment she thought her heart had stopped. He had said the 'L' word. He did. He really did. She molded herself into his arms.

"Why do you love me? Is it just for my body? Am I just an easy lay for you?"

"I don't know why, Janney. Sure, its for your body, you are so sexy. But I love you for who you are. You are, I don't know. It's complicated. You are just you. I don't know why I love you. Every time I see you, I feel like crowing, like dropping one wing and flying in circles, like killing dragons just for one smile from you. You are so wonderful. Janney, I love you, for you. I can't explain it. They don't teach us cops much about love. That must be it. They never taught me the words."

"You aren't so bad yourself, big guy," she whispered into his ear and nibbled at it with an eye tooth. Her hand wandered south. "Oh, my, you are a big boy, aren't you. What are we going to do with that monster down there?" She slowly moved herself down the bed, stopping first at his nipples. She sucked them lightly and started to slide further down when his hands found her shoulders and pulled her back up to eye level.

"I just want to lie here for a minute and gaze into your eyes, baby, before we continue. Do you mind? It really turns me on."

"Gaze all you want, James, gaze away." She fluttered her eyes at him, smiling, her heart aglow, peace in her soul.

Later when they woke again, she lay cuddled in his arms. She could still feel faint spasms of her orgasm pulsating through her. She felt so safe in James' arms. So safe; she wondered again about Volcano.

"James, are you awake?"

"Hmm."

"How are we ever going to find the 'Rose Marie'? You know the one with the rapist on board, the one I identified? We do have to find them, don't we?"

"All indications show that they are in Mexico. They are

111

out of our jurisdiction. It isn't our problem, now. We will find out all about it if they ever come back here. We have enough problems of our own. No need to try to solve Mexico's problems, too." Her good feelings left her instantly. She sat up in bed and wrapped the sheet around herself.

"Well, if you aren't going to find them, then I will. So there, you, you, you man. It may not be your problem but it is mine. I will carry the memories of what he did to me for the rest of my life. I want to see him punished. I want to see him suffer. I want to see him used like the dog he is. I want to hear him scream. I want to see all that he is, torn down and stomped into the dirt. And if you don't want to help, then I am going by myself." She trounced out of bed and ran into the bathroom.

She reappeared 20 minutes later, dressed, and ready for the world. Her hair was brushed, lipstick applied, and earrings attached. She stared at Peterson still in bed from behind the mask of her eyeliner and mascara.

"Are you going to help, or not?" One hand was on her hip, the other lay gracefully along her pantyhosed leg. She lifted her head back and stared down at him, down her nose.

He thought he had never seen a more beautiful creature. So proud, so determined, despite her inherent weakness. He imagined she looked like Joan of Arc leading the armies of France; like Madame Curie discovering Radium, like Eve rising naked from the grasslands of Eden. He knew if he let her walk out of his apartment he would lose her forever.

"Alright girl, I have some holiday time back-logged. What do you say we take the land-rover down to Mexico and see what two private citizens can do?"

"Oh, yes, James! Yes, yes, yes! It will be so much fun! Lets leave tomorrow morning!"

"Alright, I'll clear it with Maria. Make sure there is nothing I'll have to sign for the next week. Now are you coming back to bed?"

"Bed? Bed? No, way! We have too much to do! Luggage to pack, we have to make sure we have enough water. Maps! We have to be sure we have the right maps! We better get a tent, in case we get stuck out in the wilderness. Come on, lazybones! Lets go!"

'This is going to be so romantic, almost like a honeymoon,' she thought. 'And at the end of the rainbow will be that hunk, no, that god damn demon Volcano Williams.'

XXIII

At Sea Off Baja

Harv had his hands tied together in front of him with two heavy duty cable ties and then lashed to the mast compression post with a eight foot piece of rope. His feet were hobbled 6 inches apart which enabled him to get to the head and the nav table but wasn't long enough for him to get at Larry. At first, Harv had tried to talk Larry into letting them go, telling him they would drop him off on the coast or on Cedros, a large island off shore.

After five minutes of begging, and really he was begging, he had no pride left, he gave up talking to Larry. His daughter lay dead in the aft cabin. His concern now was for Janet. He didn't care if he got out of this alive, but he felt it was his duty to save Janet, to save her life. He couldn't get the picture out of his mind of his daughter laying there with a knife stuck into her heart, through her budding breast. Dead, dead on their boat. After five minutes of begging, Larry strutted, he was sure it was a strut, over to him and cut off a small piece of his ear.

"Shut up, asshole. I don't want to hear anymore from you. Keep it up and I will do your wife right in front of you. And you know the worse part? I'll make sure she enjoys it, too. At least, until the end. So just shut the fuck up."

The blood poured down the side of his head and neck before being absorbed by his shirt; and he fell into a downcast silence. 'She never had a chance at life,' he thought mournfully to himself. 'She was so full of joy and life and then to have it all extinguished in just a few seconds. By all that is good in the world, how can such things happen?' He sat down suddenly on the cabin sole. He yanked hard at his bonds, the cable ties cut into his wrists. He yanked again and again. He felt something break in his left wrist. He seemed to delight in the pain and yanked again. The pain became so intense that he lost, for a moment, the picture of his dead daughter that was haunting, stealing, eating what was left of his mind. He thought about chewing off his left wrist. He would have to be quick. The wrist would bleed badly and he had to have enough blood left to kill Larry before he lost consciousness. He would have to be quick, very quick.

Janet was steering the boat. Larry had untied her when he wanted to leave the Geronimo Island. He allowed her only her bra and panties. No where to hide a weapon, he said.

The weather was picking up; waves getting bigger; wind heeling the boat over farther and farther; and she hoped Larry was getting sicker and sicker. He was down below throwing his knife at the navigation table. It was chewing up the beautifully vanished wood. It stuck point first into the wood a distressing amount of time. So far, he seemed to be disgustingly healthy.

Jill. They had closed the companionway to the stern cabin. They hadn't wanted to do anything with her body. Even Larry didn't seem interested in touching or throwing her body overboard. No one talked about it. The boat had a dark, somber, soulless feeling after Jill's death. No one smiled. Talking was kept to a minimum. The specter of Jill's ghost was haunting them all.

Janet was not steering well. She jerked the wheel this way and that as she compensated for the wind and seas. The automatic pilot was doing a good job, but she overpowered it out of frustration. Tears flowed out of her eyes, making it difficult to see. Her mouth sagged at the corners, one shoulder was hunched over as if protecting her heart, her breath came in shallow gasps.

'Why did I throw that knife? Oh, Jill, why? How could I kill my own child? I should have realized, I should have thought, I should have known that he would move,' she thought. 'Oh, my god; oh, Jill; oh, Jill; oh, Jill; why god; oh why.' When Larry had given orders to get underway, to raise the anchor, to raise the sails, to steer south, she had obeyed like a broken, jerky robot. She felt that if she didn't think, maybe she wouldn't feel. It wasn't working. Her heart was past breaking. No, it was broken, she could feel the broken shards of it cutting away her life inside her chest. Now, she was just waiting for her body to realize it was dead. She only wanted to lie down beside her Jill, hug her for one last time, and die. She felt her life was over. She still loved her man. Harv was a good man. A very good man. Now, however, now, what kind of wife and lover could she be, with a broken, no, destroyed heart? And Harv? He loved Jill, so. Would he be able to live in the same body with his memories?

A bigger than usual wave came up from the stern. She fought the autopilot. She knew she should let it do its own thing. She knew it. The only thing was, she was so frustrated.

She was so sad. She was so destroyed. She was so terrified of what she might turn into. What kind of monster she would become. She was so, so, so empty. Her womb ached with a pain that echoed throughout her entire body.

'Oh, Jill; oh, Jill; oh, Jill; oh my God, just take me and have done with it. I killed my child. Oh, my God, I killed my child. I stuck a knife into her and killed her. I killed my one and only child. Oh, my God. Take me instead, I'm dead anyway, just take me.' She looked over the side at the endless waves, one after another, never ending. There was a kind of eternity there.

'They say that drowning is an easy way to go,' she thought, 'as long as you don't fight it. Force all the air out of your lungs, open your mouth wide, and inhale water in a big gasp. That way there was only a brief moment of choking, then the lungs keep working pumping the water in and out, thinking it was air, and then I'll slowly fade away.' She practiced forcing the air out of her lungs. Seeing how much air she could get out. 'If I could get rid of the air first and then dive in, head first, I could inhale water right away and not fight it.' She watched the seas, the eternal waves. The endless ocean. 'It wouldn't be too bad. One quick gasp and then fade away.' And the pain, the pain would fade away, too. And it would be over. It would be over. Her life would be over. Her life would be over. 'Oh, my God. Save me, oh, please, God, please, please save me. Jesus, save me. Mary, Mary, forgive me, please forgive me for killing my child, my child, my Jill.' She collapsed to her knees by the wheel. She was sobbing so hard it was hard for her to breathe.

She heard a small sound, like wood sliding on wood very slowly. She looked vaguely, despairingly around for the source. She hoped it wasn't the mast.

'That's all I need right now, to lose the mast,' she thought. 'Maybe it will fall and hit my head, and kill me instantly. Oh, yes. God kill me. Send me to hell where I belong. Let me burn for all eternity.'

"Hey, up there. Who's steering? Get back on course, damn it." Larry smiled to himself. He was becoming a real sea dog. He even talked like one. He didn't feel seasick at all, as long as he didn't move. He lay on one berth, on his back, his knife close to his hand

"I didn't tell you to look around. Steer this boat straight. If I get seasick from your bad steering you are going to regret it, lady. You are going to really regret it, I kid you not. Unless, you are trying to get me sick?" He climbed out of the cabin and into the cockpit. He reached over the wheel and ran his fingers through the small hairs at the base of her neck. He tugged at them forcing her head back. He leaned over her, smelling her breath, looked into her eyes.

"Yeah, you'll live." Even though he was pulling against her small hairs, hard, she felt no pain. She felt him lower his head to her neck and his warm breath flooded over her throat, his teeth scraped against the pulsing artery there. Despite herself and to her horror, she felt her nipples start to harden. He looked again into her eyes.

"Yeah, you'll be alright. You still got some life in you. Don't do anything stupid out here, OK. I need you to get this crate into some safe port, alright? No hurting yourself till we anchor, promise? Besides, if you want to off yourself, I know lots of interesting ways." His eyes gleamed and he lowered his head again and sucked at the skin, in the hollow of her neck, just above her collarbone with his lips. To her disgust, she felt her shoulders relax, her chest inflate and her back arch. As he pulled away, still sucking, her eyes blazed at him. She stared at him with bared teeth, lips pulled back into a thin line, fists, white, clenching the wheel.

"Keep your hands off me, guy. Keep your fucking hands off me."

He smiled down at her. "Let that anger burn, baby. Let that anger burn bright. There's nothing so healthy as a bit of anger when you start wondering what it is all about." With a little smile he went down below.

She heard the noise again. Careful to keep on course she looked around. She looked aft for anything moving around, sliding around, making a noise on deck. She noticed that the stern hatch had slid open some how. She turned back to the wheel to make sure of her course and then reached back to close the hatch. A pair of blue pixie eyes, sparkling with life, framed with tousled blond hair were suddenly peeking over the stern hatch combing.

'Oh, fine. I am going crazy. I'm seeing ghosts. What next? How much more must I suffer? How much, dear God, how much? Am I in hell already?'

Janet turned back forward to watch her course and then felt a little tug on her panties. She swiveled, mouth open, looking back aft. The blue twinkling eyes now owned a mouth and a finger was held across it, motioning silence. The eyes were jumping up and down in their sockets, in happiness and joy of life. The mouth twitched, trying to speak, held back by her own finger pressed against her lips.

Janet abandoned the wheel. Her hands covered her face; her eyes wide, she stared at her daughter between her spread fingers, her whole body was shaking. She reached over to Jill and grabbed her and hugged her and hugged her and hugged her. Her hand dove inside Jill's blouse, feeling her left breast and came out with wads and wads of money. Janet looked at the money in astonishment. She looked back inside Jill's blouse, tearing at her clothes. There must have been six inches of money in there. She tore out the money, scattering it, till she reached Jill's skin. It was unblemished.

"Dad said we had to give the money back," she whispered, "but I say we fought for it so I think we should be able to keep it and anyway I found it first, so finder's keepers," Jill whispered into her mother's ear. "I know I am supposed to obey Dad but he can be so silly at times not that it is his fault as he is only a man not a woman like us so we can't blame him, so I was really just protecting him when I took all the money out of the valise and pushed it everywhere I could hide it, in my shirt, in my pants!" She showed her mother her pockets, full of money. There was even money stuffed and flowing out of her socks.

"I had to pretend to be dead for the longest time and then I fell asleep and it isn't true what they say, sleeping on a bed of money is really lumpy but I slept anyway and now we have lots of money and Sir Daddy can buy the new windless he always pretended he didn't want, isn't it wonderful to be a woman? We woman are so smart and..."

Janet pushed a still whispering Jill down into the stern cabin with a hand on top of her head. She quietly closed the hatch and turned back to the wheel. With a gasp she saw Larry watching her from the forward cabin hatch.

"What the fuck was I just telling you, bitch? Steer the fucking boat. And stop talking to yourself. You are keeping me awake. Damn stupid woman. Sharpen up. Or else!"

XXIV

Ashore on the Baja Peninsula

Janney shoved the last bit of camping gear into the back of the land rover. She stood back with her hands on her hips and looked at the load with satisfaction. There wasn't a space left to fit a toothpick.

"James, the car is packed. We are ready. Let's go!" Peterson wasn't very enthusiastic about their chances of even seeing any boat at sea while driving down a road in the middle of the Baja, but he was enthusiastic about getting Janney away from the maddening crowds, restaurants, cities, and civilization, full stop. He wanted to get to know the real Janney, not the face that she put on for people to see. He was getting very interested in her, more and more each day, but his cop's caution was a leash that held him back until he was sure.

If they were to have a life together, he wanted to share everything with her, but he couldn't until he was positive about her. He even had her checked out, just to be sure she wasn't a plant sent in by the cartels. She was clean, bar an arrest for possession when she was fifteen. It was only a few grams and somehow she got off with only a warning; rich parents, he assumed.

Peterson made sure everything was running smoothly at the office before he left. Maria made a big thing about it. She had baked a cake with a big dick shaped candle. She gave him a going away present, a box of condoms with the tips cut off. Her eyes glowed as he left. She was very proud that he was dating. Maria gave Janney a well leafed copy of, 'The Joy of Sex'.

The border wasn't any problem as they crossed into Mexico. It never was, going south into Mexico. Coming back north into the USA would be another story. They stopped at a panderia for some boleos and cookies in Ensenada and scanned the harbor for the 'Rose Marie'. Immigration and the Port Captain were right. She wasn't in port.

They tried to keep to the coastal road but it often went miles inland to avoid the lagoons common in this part of the world. Eventually they ended up at the little town of San

Quentin without seeing any sailboats much less the 'Rose Marie'. Janney was a little depressed from their lack of success. As they pulled up to a motel and Janney started to get out, Peterson started the car again.

"Listen; let's camp out on the beach. A friend told me it is a beautiful beach and it is going to be a cloudless night. What do you say?" Janney looked a bit doubtful.

"They say it is dangerous to camp on beaches in Mexico. They say there are gangs of banditos wandering around Baja."

"Don't forget, you have a cop sharing the tent with you, plus we can keep an eye out for the Rose Marie in case she comes in to anchor in the bay."

"Yes! Yes, let's do it. Oh, this trip is going to be so romantic!" She hugged her arms around her shoulders and then grabbed Peterson and kissed him and then stared into his eyes.

"This is going to be a great trip, James. I just know it, I do. I think this is a trip that we will remember for the rest of our lives."

Just at dusk, they set up camp on a wide pure white sand beach. Small waves crashed ashore on the vaguely horseshoe shaped bay. Seagulls cried along the deserted coast. Not a person or a building could be seen. Together they ran down the wet sand, hand in hand, crying back at the seagulls, laughter in their hearts, in their voices, in their souls. Peterson tackled Janney and they fell into the shallow water kissing, hands wandering. Janney wrestled with Peterson. He managed to get her on top of him, with her hands pinning his upper arms.

"What's that, James?" Janney pointed down the beach towards a dark hump and what looked like a sand fight; sand was flying everywhere. He sat up suddenly, an arm around her to keep her from flying backwards.

"Let's find out. Come on." They raced down the beach and then slowed as they neared, mouths agape, eyes wide with wonder.

"She only has one back leg, I mean, flipper. Oh, the poor thing. Let's help her, Honey." There in front of them was a giant turtle laying eggs into a hole in the sand. As they walked up, she started filling in the hole but was having a hard time doing it as her right back flipper was mostly gone. It looked like, from the scar, that she had been attacked by a shark.

Most of the sand from her one flipper was missing the hole, entirely. Her eyes were wet from tears and her motions were getting slower and slower as she tired.

They quietly crawled up and helped the mother fill in the hole. The turtle looked at them for a moment and then went back to her work. She kept flinging sand, most of it ended on top of Peterson and Janney. They smiled at each other and kept working. Finally the eggs were covered and the hole filled. The mother inspected their work and then satisfied crawled back into the water and was gone.

They watched the darkening sea and the deep reds and blues of the sunset above it for ten minutes still lying on the sand by the egg nest, and then he took Janney by the hand, pulled her to her feet and they walked back to their camp in silence. Halfway there, Peterson's eyes started to tear up. Drops flowed from his eyes as he walked along, but he was smiling. As he stumbled on an unseen rock, Janney grabbed his shoulders and made him sit down on the sand.

"What is wrong, honey? What is wrong, James?" Peterson didn't reply. He let the tears fall from his face unabated.

"At last, I have a great memory," he said almost to himself, staring out to sea, staring out to the island of San Martin disappearing in the dark. "I have a final, really great memory at last." He dried his tears and they made love, there on the sand, on a lovely beach, under the stars, seen only by the distant peak of the pirate island of Sir Francis Drake.

XXV

Sailing down the Baja Coast

The 'Rose Marie' was coasting along the tall island of Cedros. She was sheltered from the Pacific swells by the island and the boat ghosted along quietly under her full set of shroud-like white sails. Ashore sea lion and elephant seal males fought for breeding rights with tremendous roars and flashing teeth as they gathered their separate harems on isolated patches of beach.

Aboard the boat Harv fought against his bonds, fought to regain mastery of his vessel, fought to be the alpha male in their little floating world. There was only one female left for the two men. Harv was sure Larry had designs on Janet. He was determined to stop him.

The death of his daughter had broken his spirit. The kind, rational man that he had been, had died with Jill. Now all he felt was the need for revenge. All he wanted was to kill. If the world could kill his daughter, if the world operated by killing, killing when ever it wanted, then damn it, he was going to be a killer, too. He had been wrong his whole life. He had always tried to do the right thing. Now he just wanted revenge. Now he just wanted what was good for himself, good for the memory of his daughter.

Jill would never have died it Larry hadn't pirated their boat. His family would be having a wonderful cruise exploring Mexico, walking down endless beaches, eating at quaint little cafes, drinking Pacificos while sitting on the beach watching the sunset. They would be having the dream cruise Harv had dreamed of for so many years. It was Larry's fault, Larry's fault. All Larry's fault. Larry had to die. Harv nodded his head to himself. Larry had to die, die, die. Larry was responsible for all that was wrong in the world. It would be a wonderful world without Larry. Larry had to die. And he was going to kill him.

Harv had pulled against his bonds until he had lost feeling in his left hand. He had broken or dislocated something in there. He could feel the bones grate against each other when he tried to move it. Not that he could move the hand very much; he seemed to be loosing any use of it. Not that he cared. He only needed one hand to kill.

When he saw Larry kissing Janet out in the cockpit, forcing her spine back, her chest in the air, her head back, her mouth sagging open, her fingers spread achingly open, arms falling back from her shoulders, he pulled against his bonds again and again and again. Very, very hard; frustrated and angry at being helpless while his woman was being mauled, fueled his fury of being tied up like a chicken going to the slaughter house. Frustrated at having his dream sailing cruise turned into a horror movie. Frustrated at being unable to protect his family against a much younger man. Angry that the onset of age had stolen the man he once was. His kind eyes became riddled with red streaks. His laughter lines around his eyes disappeared and his face elongated as his jaw opened slightly as if getting ready to bite.

He yanked and pulled at his bonds. The bones in his left hand dislocated but still he yanked. He didn't care how much it hurt. The agony of the bones grinding away in the inside of his hand had dulled into an ache, now. Finally he felt his left hand slip out a bit from the cable tie. He looked at the thin thing that once had been a hand in astonishment and then quickly brought it up to his neck and covered it in the blood still dripping from his cut ear. His hands became slipperier and slipperier. He pulled again and then his useless left hand was free. The hand was narrow, formless, like it had been crushed into a single digit. With the extra space left in the cable tie bond, his right hand came out easily and he quickly untied his ankles. A weapon; he needed a weapon. He opened his tool locker and holding his useless, aching, tortured left hand close to his chest, he shuffled though the assorted tools, discarding screwdrivers, pliers, wrenches, till he found a ball peen hammer. He made a few practice swings and then suddenly Larry was coming down the stairs. He darted into the galley and held his hammer high ready to bury it deep into Larry's skull.

With one glance, as he went below, Larry saw Harv had slipped his bonds. He instantly jack knifed his head back into the cockpit, barely missing Harv's speeding hammer. Larry jumped back down below, skidded forward to the mast, and turned to face Harv, his knees bent, his hands open, his eyes shining in anticipation of combat, his face spread with a little smile, and he laughed. Harv, having missed Larry's head had been unable to stop the momentum of the hammer. It had buried itself in the formica of the galley counter. He was pulling at it trying to free the hammer, but it was stuck. The head was buried deep in the wood under the formica. Harv tried to use his deformed left hand to help pull it out. It was no use.

Larry danced forward with unequal steps, like a cobra he darted this way and that. Finally he thrust forward and hit Harv hard with the base of his palm just between the nose and the cheekbone, above the teeth, below the eye. Harv dropped like a stone; the nerve endings in his face had fired their synapses all together overloading his brain which shut down to protect itself. He stood above Harv, looked at the useless left hand, the unconscious man, he looked over at the bloody cable tie and shook his head.

"You have got a lot of guts, guy. You have got way too many guts for any normal man. Jesus, Harv; look what you did to yourself. What the fuck am I supposed to do with you now?" He knew he couldn't force himself to tie Harv up again. "Christ, if I keep tying you up, you are going to end up a fucking cripple." He looked at the hand again. "Even more of a cripple."

Janet was glad when Larry left her. Her body was still trembling as he walked towards the hatch. She didn't know if it was from anger or her body's response to Larry's touch.

"Fucking asshole," she murmured to herself and looked around for something to hit him with. Her eyes fell a winch handle sticking out of the top of the port winch. It was a heavy piece of stainless steel with a handle at one end and a bulb which had a square piece of metal sticking out that attached into the top of the winch. It looked like a very dangerous weapon. She lifted it and balanced it in her hand. She guessed it weighed about 10 pounds. Suddenly the sounds of laughter came from down below; Larry's laughter. What was he doing to her Harv now? With a surge she twisted around the wheel over to the hatch and dropped herself down to the floor below. She landed on the pads of her feet and saw Larry standing over her unconscious husband, laughing. A red film clouded her vision and her body was still trembling, nevertheless she softly walked towards Larry who looked up in interest.

"When I told you to let your anger burn bright, girl, I didn't mean for you to do something stupid." He looked at her up and down. "In fact, I did tell you not to do anything stupid, didn't I?"

Janet didn't seem to hear him. She rushed at him; her winch handle raised up and swung it at him. He responded like a matador. He slipped to one side and let her momentum carry her forward. He turned facing forward watching her with amusement in his eyes. He smiled his little smile, then reached out suddenly and tore her bra off of her. She was still avoiding his eyes. She looked anywhere but his eyes. Her winch handle still raised high in one hand, the other arm protecting her breasts.

"You know you want it, girl. You know your body needs it. Don't look away. No one is going to know. Your man is going to be under for another hour at the very least. Come here, girl. Come here," he commanded.

She gathered her feet under her, and then rushed towards him swinging her handle right at his face, right at his intolerable eyes.

She felt the handle hit the trim around the bookcase on the port side. The wood splintered and split and the beautiful varnished case was destroyed. She looked in dismay at the wood, forgetting Larry for a second, wood that she had spent weeks applying fifteen coats of varnish to, destroyed in seconds. Tears gathered in her eyes. She felt his hand touch her shoulder. Again she swung her winch handle, again he stepped aside. As she missed he pushed her forward. She fell, spinning. She landed on her hands and knees.

When she twisted over on her back, his eyes no longer held humor in their depths. Now there was the fire of desire burning inside of them. His face was hard; his aura was dangerous and powerful. She scrambled, crab like, away still on her back, he reached forward, with flared nostrils, and stripped her panties off of her. Horror spread over her face, fear clouded her eyes. His hand flickered forward again and then her handle was torn from her hand. He stared at her womanhood and then licked his lips. She had shaven herself as a present for Harv. Now there was nothing down there to protect her from prying eyes.

She made the mistake of looking into his eyes. She was suddenly frozen. She just stared at him, a bird entranced by a snake. Her legs started to tremble. He tore his shirt off, pulling it over his head. He started to undo his belt buckle, never taking his eyes off of her, when suddenly he stood upright and with out a word fell flat on his face at her feet. Behind him stood Jill, pure flashing anger flaring in waves over her face, and out of Larry's back, stuck deep into his back, erupted the spear from Jill's Hawaiian sling.

XXVI

Puebla of Turtle Bay

Raoul had tired of Turtle Bay. He and his rabble army had stolen everything of value they could find. He burned both sailboats he had found in the harbor after stripping them bare. Half of their illicit haul his men had played with, then tiring of it, destroyed it. They had found far too much beer, too much to ever drink in the few days they were in town. They loaded as much as they could on donkeys. Raoul didn't believe in cars and trucks anymore.

"All they do is run out of gas, and then all the federales have to do is follow the line of dead trucks. Then they have us. It is better to disappear into the desert. In the desert they will never find us with their planes and satellites. There are too many shadows in the desert, too many caves, too many cliffs. The desert is not a place a civilized man will go. Good thing we not civilized, ay amigos?"

He had toyed with the town. He didn't burn it and kill every living thing as he often did. He liked the town. It was far from anywhere else. There was little chance of the army coming to protect such a little place. It was rich from the selling of lobsters, and now, more important, they were in terror of him.

"Next time, me amigos, when we come to town, they will bow to us. They will bring us all their good things; they will strip the most beautiful women naked and bring them to us in chains. They will have a fiesta just for us. Ay, amigos, this is our town, now!"

The dead in the streets had disappeared, buried in secret by the survivors in a mass grave. The raped and abused, the tortured and the maimed hid under beds and in closets. Waiting, hoping to see another tomorrow.

Peterson and Janney had left San Quentin early that morning and drove down the central highway to get around

Scammon`s and Black Warrior lagoons, breeding grounds that Grey Whales used after migrating from the Arctic, and then cut back for the coast on a small road that led to a small fishing town on the coast that yachts often called into called, Turtle Bay. Janney hoped they would find the 'Rose Marie' there or someone who had seen her. They had the CD player on and were singing along together in unison with the Moody Blues. Outside the air conditioned land rover, cactus and desert abounded. Peterson wondered what men had built this road. They must have been as tough as nails to live and work in such a climate. As they neared the town they came upon a group of desperados and Peterson sped up to get past them.

_/)_/)_/)

Raoul sat on a burro and peered into the windows of the passing vehicle and saw a beautiful woman with the most remarkable grey eyes. He took out his jar of eyes filled with formaldehyde and swirled it about. He had blues of every different shade, browns in a variety of sizes and hues, some really nice black ones, even a rare pink one. No, he was right. He didn't have a grey eye. He especially didn't have a grey eye from such a beauty. He wanted her eyes. 'After all,' he whispered to himself, 'if a man didn't have a quest in this world, then he wasn't much of a man.'

XXVII

Aboard the 'Rose Marie'

Larry lay there on the floor. The Hawaiian sling had three separate spear points. It was designed that way to paralyze the fish so it wouldn't struggle and get off the spear. It seemed to have stopped Larry.

"Wow, that really worked good! You know, I didn't really believe it when they showed us that video on how to use this spear in the store, that the fish would just die, but look I just killed my first pirate! At least I think he is dead. Dad. Is Larry dead? Wake up, Dad! Mom? What's wrong with Dad? Mom, why are you naked? You are going to catch your death of cold if you run around like that. Mom? Why are you crying? Why isn't everybody congratulating me? I just saved everyone!"

Janet crawled over to Harv. He was still alive. She was very careful with his ruined hand. She laid him flat on his back and arranged his hand on his chest. Then she went to Larry. Blood was flowing freely from the spear points. She remembered from somewhere that if the blood was still flowing the victim wasn't dead.

"Jill, find me another of those cable ties, quickly. Larry isn't dead. We have to tie him up again before he comes to. Quickly Jill!"

"Mom, I don't know where he got those things. Let's tie him up with ropes. I know lots of good knots!"

Janet quickly found some clothes from her lockers. She didn't know why she had to be dressed to tie up a pirate, but it seemed to be important to her, so she followed her instincts. Jill was back soon with a long piece of line and they had Larry was trussed up like a turkey invited to Thanksgiving.

Janet rushed up on deck to check on the course of the 'Rose Marie'. She had passed the end of the island and was meeting the Pacific swells again. The rolling of the boat couldn't be good for Harv. He could be seriously injured. She had to get the boat into harbor somewhere hopefully with a hospital and police. She jumped down to the Nav desk and pulled out the Marine chart of Baja. There was a place called Turtle Bay 20 miles further down the coast. She recalled Harv talking about it. She thought she remembered him saying that it had good protection and was a nice little town. It certainly looked like a protected port on the chart. It was almost totally land locked.

"Jill, be sure to tie up his feet, too. And prop some pillows around your father so he won't move in the swells."

"OK, Mom. Can I tie a hangman's noose around the pirate's head? My sailing instructor showed us how to tie one when the boys weren't paying attention. They sure wanted to learn knots after that! But remember Joey? He tied nooses around all his sister's dolls and hung them from lamps in her room, so our instructor had to stop showing us all the neat knots. When is Dad going to wake up? Dad? Are you awake?"

"Jill, leave him alone. He is very tired and he will wake up when he is ready." 'At least I hope so. Oh, Harv; please be

OK,' she prayed to herself. Janet took the wheel and steered southwest to round Punta Eugenia, the last obstacle before they began their run into Turtle Bay. She hoped there was some kind of medical care there. Harv should have been awake by now. She hoped he hadn't fallen into a coma or was dying.

'Oh, my God, please don't be dying, Harv. I love you so much, I need you, Harv. Don't die Harv. Please,' she prayed to herself. She left the wheel for a second and dashed over to the companionway. Harv was still not moving. She saw that Larry was making small movements. She could see his hands trying to get to the spear in his back. Quickly she rushed down into the cabin. For a second she thought about pushing the spear further into him, hoping to kill him, but in the end she pulled it out and took it with her back into the cockpit. She felt its balance and weight with satisfaction. She felt much better armed.

"Jill? Jill, keep away from Larry. I think he is coming to. What ever you do, don't let him get his hands on you. Jill, Where are you, Jill?" She looked down below. She couldn't see Jill anywhere. "JILL!"

"What Mom?" said Jill as she came up from the stern hatch. "You always tell me never to scream. And here you are screaming away and Sir Daddy is trying to sleep. Really, Mom, you have to try to become a better adult. Now, Dad, you and I both know that he will always be a little boy inside a man's body. It isn't his fault. He just grew up to be a male instead of a female like us girls. Isn't that right, Mom? Mom? Mom, are you listening to me?"

"Honey, just stay up here in the cockpit with me. I need your help going into the port. I need you to watch, to watch for, for buoys? Yes, Jill. Watch out for buoys, it is very important we find the buoys. So important that you can't go down below for even a second. OK?"

"Mom, I got it. You want to keep me away from the pirate. Don't worry. I'm the one who speared him. I saved you, both. Yep. I saved the day. The cavalry came riding out of the sun and speared the pirate right in the back. Yep, would have speared him right between the eyes but it was a sneak attack. Good thing I was here or he would have made the two of you walk the plank. Yep. I saved the day. Mom, why are you crying?"

XXVIII

Town of Turtle Bay

When Peterson and Janney drove into Turtle Bay they were struck by how abandoned the place looked. No one was in the streets; no one even looked out of any windows. It was like a ghost town. They arrived at the harbor and found one boat burned to the waterline and another just awash, tied to the dock.

"Come on, Janney; let's find out what boats these two are. Can you recognize them?"

"This town really spooks me out. I get a feeling that something really, really bad happened here. And it happened not too long ago. Do you feel anything?"

"My kind of law enforcement relies on facts, Ma'am, just the facts." He looked at her with an eyebrow raised. "Don't tell me you never watched reruns of Dragnet?" He faked a look of astonishment.

"See? We really don't know much about each other. That's why spending time like this is so important. Take ghost towns like this. It could be from the set of the Twilight Zone, or The Magnificent Seven. Which one would you pick?"

"Me? I'd say 'Waterworld', personally, Ma'am. Either that or 'The Day the Earth Stood Still'. The place looks old enough for that. And look at this boat." They had reached the end of the dock and were gazing down at a wreck of a sailboat. The hatches were torn off, portholes seemed to have bullet holes in them, and marine gear was thrown out and around everywhere. A strange smell seemed to penetrate the air. "Do you think this might be the 'Rose Marie', Janney?"

"No, she is too long and the 'Rose Marie' is a ketch, and has a red stripe the length of her waterline."

"Ketch, two masts, then," Peterson murmured. "Then that boat over there couldn't be her either, could it?"

"I certainly hope not," she said looking at the wreck bobbing in the small waves hitting the sandy beach. "What happened here? It looks like the end of the world."

"We might have some answers over there." He pointed over to a tree to the east of the dock. A man was standing there, looking out to sea. He wasn't looking for anything. He was just staring, lost in his own world, lost in his memories.

They walked back along the dock and transversed the beach.

"Excuse me, Sir. I wonder if we might have a word with you. Have you seen a ketch rigged, 32 footer, with a red stripe called the 'Rose Marie'?" The man continued to stare out at sea. He didn't seem to be aware of them at all. Janney reached out and touched his arm. He jumped back in shock and then grabbed Janney, both hands on the upper arms.

"Run, Senora, run, rapido, muy rapido. They will come back, si Senora, they will come back to kill all of us. You must run!" He gave her a little push and then fell to his knees, hands holding his face, as sobs racked his back and shoulders. Janney knelt down beside him and tried to comfort him, but he sank back into his own world and stared again out at the endless sea.

"James, look." She pointed at what looked to be a dead body further down the beach. They walked down towards it. The closer
they got, the more it seemed that it was a body. It was on its stomach, if it was a body. Janney started to lag back, only continuing because she didn't want to let go of Peterson's hand.

It was a body. A naked man. Peterson grabbed hold of an arm and rolled the body over. Intestines had spurted out of the belly and sand crabs had made their way into the body cavity where they were feasting. Shocked, Peterson let the arm go and mercifully the body rolled back onto its stomach. Janney hid her eyes in Peterson's neck, holding on to him with both arms, while moaning in pitiful cries. He picked her up, one arm under her legs, one under her shoulders, her face still in his neck and carried her inland away from the water.

It wasn't far till he saw another naked body. Again, a male, a rope had been tied around his sexual organs so tightly that the scrotum had burst. A section of rebar was shoved up the body's rectum till it exited out of its mouth. Peterson kept Janney's head against his neck, hiding the body, and took her back to the car. He gently deposited her in the passenger seat of the rover and reached over her to his police band radio.

"Any law enforcement personnel, this is an American police officer in Turtle Bay reporting a double homicide. Any law enforcement personnel, this is a United States of America police officer reporting a double homicide in the town of Turtle Bay." Only static replied to his transmissions. He cursed himself for not taking Spanish courses when they were offered by the department. He knew people in Europe commonly spoke four or five foreign languages.

'Hell, I can barely speak English,' he joked to himself. "Janney, Honey? Honey, I need you to try to contact someone on the radio. Don't give up. Keep trying. You never know when propagation will improve." He stroked her head like he would a cat as she reached for the microphone. He gazed around. They were in a bowl. High hills surrounded them. 'Not much of a chance for a signal to get over those hills,' he thought to himself. 'But it will keep her mind off the bodies.'

"Listen, Janney, I am going to take a quick look around, try to see what happened and then we'll go for help. Keep trying on the radio, OK, Honey?"

He started to search the rest of the town, but then on second thought he went to the overloaded back of the rover and pulled out a shotgun. He broke open an ammo box and loaded the gun alternating solid shot with buckshot. Then he reached down into a well hidden secret locker in a wheel well and pulled out a .357 magnum. He checked to make sure he had a full load, set the safety and then stuffed the gun down between his belt and his spine. He pulled his shirt over his belt, to hide the gun, and started his search. He took one last look at Janney calling on the radio. She waved at him through the open door of the vehicle.

She couldn't get the thought of the man who was tortured to death out of her brain. She wished it was that Volcano on the ground, dead. She wished it was she who had shoved the rebar in and in and in. She wanted so much to see him cry, to see him beg for mercy. She wanted to hear him say, 'Please, stop. It hurts. Please, no more.' She wanted to hear him say it, and then she wanted to shove it in even harder. She wanted him punished for what he had done to her. She wanted to do the punishing. Especially if he had done anything to that little girl.

Years ago, when she was a teenager, she had been inducted into a gang. It wasn't as if she had much choice. It was join or live a life in hell on the way to school and back. They had made her into a mule, transporting dope around the city. One of the Lieutenants of the gang had it in for her. Every chance he got he was always feeling her up. Sometimes she wished she had been born plain looking. Maybe then she would be allowed to live in peace.

She had skimmed a gram here and a gram there from her shipments and eventually put it all into the Lieutenant's pocket just before a big meet. She had stood up just before the meet started and, even though she was quaking so hard her knees were knocking, she had managed to get it out that she knew who had been stealing from the gang. When she had all of their attention, she just pointed at the lieutenant. She didn't trust her voice to say anything. They found the dope in his pocket and beat him to death, in front of her. They used baseball bats and broke every bone in his body. When they were finished, it wasn't a body anymore. No one could ever recognize it as a human body. A blob of meat, maybe. Something a mad dog would turn up its nose at.

That's what she wanted to do to that Volcano. That would teach him a lesson. But she wondered if when she came face to face with him if she wouldn't come under his spell again. Become his robot, his mule, his woman, and loving it. Never. She was too strong. And she had Peterson with her. The man she loved. Not like that bastard. She would make him suffer.

That is what she wanted to happen to that Volcano guy. For what he did to her. Sure, she had enjoyed it, at first, a little bit. Well, maybe, a lot. But he just kept doing it and doing it, over and over, using every different part of her body, things she had never even heard of before. Whenever she tried to stop him, he just did something to her. She didn't know what. It was like he sucked the will out of her. Like he sucked the Janney out of her. Like he just wanted a body. Nothing more. He didn't want her. He just wanted a piece of meat to use. She wanted him to pay for that. And she wanted to do the collecting. She wanted him to suffer. She wanted to stick her thumb in his belly button while he was screaming in agony. And James was just the man to help her do it. Just the man to hold him down as she did it.   Never. She was too strong. And she had Peterson with her. The man she loved. Not like that bastard. She would make him suffer.

That is what she wanted to happen to that Volcano guy. For what he did to her. Sure, she had enjoyed it, at first, a little bit. Well, maybe, a lot. But he just kept doing it and doing it, over and over, using every different part of her body, things she had never even heard of before. Whenever she tried to stop him, he just did something to her. She didn't know what. It was like he sucked the will out of her. Like he sucked the Janney out of her. Like he just wanted a body. Nothing more. He didn't want her. He just wanted a piece of meat to use.

She wanted him to pay for that. And she wanted to do the collecting. She wanted him to suffer. She wanted to stick her thumb in his belly button while he was screaming in agony. And James was just the man to help her do it. Just the man to hold him down as she did it.

XXIX

Aboard the 'Rose Marie'

Larry slowly came to. Again he just lay there and sensed his surroundings. The sea was rougher now; he could feel bigger waves hit the boat. Janet and Jill seemed to be up on deck. He could hear them talking about buoys, or channels or some such sailor shit. The man? He couldn't hear Harv at all. He wondered if he had killed him when he went for the nerve ganglions in the face. It was potentially a kill spot, but he had never managed to hit it just right before. Not for lack of trying. A man had to keep in practice.

Slowly he became aware of an ache in his back, just above the kidneys. As he thought about it, the pain suddenly became more intense. Waves of agony crashed though his body and then reflected again and again. The pain, now that he recognized it, was incredibly acute. Every muscle in his body clenched in agony. He took a deep breath and accepted the pain. He calmed his mind. He stopped fighting it, stopped thinking about it, tried to accept the pain as something normal, as just a sensation. Like the taste of sugar.

Slowly the pain faded and he became aware he was trussed up like a turkey. He felt his bonds. Clothesline. He smiled his little smile. 'Clothesline,' he thought, 'damn amateurs.'

For years he had let the nail on his left thumb grow as long as it wanted. Once a week he sharpened it into a triangular point, till its tip was as sharp as a knife. It was a

133

very useful adaptation. It made shoplifting a breeze. With one twist of his thumb any package was open and the goods shaken out and separated from the magnetic security device. It was easy to keep what he was doing out of sight of the eye sky camera. The cameras always looked for someone with two hands on the package. Not him.

He had never been a talented pickpocket. He didn't like it. He didn't like taking from people, just companies, businesses, businesses with big overbearing bosses. But when funds were low and the stomach was empty, a man had to do what he had to do. He didn't like it but with a swipe of his thumb through the material of a pocket, it was a lot easier. The wallet just fell into his hand. The mark? He probably thought he ripped his pants on something. Whatever, he didn't fucking give a shit.

Slowly he let his eyes open, just a slit. Promptly but slowly he closed them again. He was on the cabin floor and Harv was on the berth just above him. He listened for breathing. Nothing there. He opened his eyes again and looked around. He couldn't see the woman in the cockpit from his position, but it was no trouble hearing her. Them. Sounded like the little girl had been faking it. Like women everywhere, they were jabbering away. With a few deft swipes with his thumb, his hands were free. In a matter of seconds his legs were released. He smiled at all the rope lying around him. Must have been the little girl. Felt like her handiwork. She had definitely not spared any rope.

He checked Harv. He was alive but just barely. 'Good,' he thought, 'one less complication.' He grabbed some of the longer pieces of rope and started to tie up Harv but as he touched the ruined left hand he stopped.

"This character isn't going to be much trouble with a hand like that." He whispered to himself. He felt his back again and his hand came back covered in blood.

'They shot me!' he thought in astonishment. Then he thought again. It didn't feel like a gunshot. It felt more like multiple knife wounds; wounds that didn't go too deep.

'Must have been the little girl, damn but she is a firecracker. Too bad she will have to be punished. Can't have people shoving a shiv in me and walking away. Bad for the reputation.' Too bad, he really liked Jill, he liked her spunk.

He heard cheering up on deck. The little girl was shouting, "We made it, yay, Mom!" And the sound of an anchor and chain running off the deck. He peeked out a port hole.

They were anchored next to a town!

"Finally I can get off this hell ship! These people are really crazy. You'd think they would be scared, guy like me coming into their lives, but, no, they fight back every time I turn away for a second. These sailors are crazy people," he murmured to himself. "I need a weapon. Something to scare those two wildcats into submission." He looked around the cabin. Nothing. He had thrown every available weapon overboard. He found a butter knife in a drawer. "I guess this will have to do."

He peeked out the companionway. The little girl had climbed up the mast for some unknown reason and Janet was standing by the mast trying to talk her into coming down. They were too far away to grab. He needed to take them by surprise. He didn't want to hurt the family any more than he had too. Not anymore, not now when he was almost off the boat. He looked at Harv. Maybe he finally got that face jab just right. He was still dead to the world.

"Even if you are dying, I can use you one more time." He reached down and pulled Harv up by the armpits and dragged him up the steps and into the cockpit. He felt something open in his back and blood start to pour more quickly out of his wound. He sat down on the seat, put his butter knife to Harv's throat, and waited for them to find him.

XXX

Puebla of Turtle Bay

Raoul turned his gang around and rode back into town. He smiled to himself. Just when they thought they were through with him, here he is coming back again.

'The truth is,' he thought to himself, 'I am starting to feel horny again, my balls, they feel full of puss and blood. Time to find a woman again. Especially one with grey eyes. Beautiful grey eyes.'

"El Jefe, there is nothing in the village, Senor. We have

taken everything, Senor; we have even taken all the tortillas. Why do we go back, El Jefe?" Enrique looked at Raoul with puzzlement on his drunk face. He was a little nervous. He knew how strong El Jefe was. No one knew why. 'Must have been something to do with ape ancestors or something', he thought with a smile 'Maybe his father was an ape and his mother a baboon,' he whispered to himself.

"We go because I say we go, stupido! And what the fuck are you smiling about? What the fuck did you just say?'"

"But, Senor, why," Raoul whipped a straight razor out of his boot where he kept it in the hollow created between his Achilles' tendon and his ankle bone, reached over as quick as an asp and sliced the corner of Enrique's mouth. He would never smile again. Enrique then made a mistake. He reached into his pocket for the pistol that he still carried from the yacht. As soon as his hand reached for the gun, Raoul went into action.

He leaned from the burro and feinted a slice for the throat, as Enrique's arm came up in defense, Raoul cut down from the back of the armpit to the stomach in between the fifth and sixth ribs four inches deep, burying the straight razor and ripping down. The razor made a hissing, snakelike sound as it sliced through cloth, skin and viscera effortlessly. Enrique fell into shock immediately. As he gasped in pain his left lung filled with blood and guts and he coughed up blood. The heart struggled against no blood pressure and enormous shock, spurted for a few seconds then thankfully lay still. Raoul kicked at the dead body.

"We go to the town," Raoul didn't look at what was left of his gang, but he did keep his ears open. As he heard their footsteps following his burro he smiled to himself. They feared him. He loved being feared. He loved making these big people obey him, him with his little body, He felt around the crotch of his pants till he found his little organ. Yes, he felt himself getting hard. As hard as it ever got.

'Si, my little grey eyed beauty. Your death is going to be a thing of legends. I wonder how many body parts I can cut off before you die.' He thought of her, armless, legless, without breasts or ears or nose. He would leave her beautiful grey eyes for last. He looked down and smiled in the general direction of his little semi-hard erection, barely as big as a thumb, and he kicked the burro into a semblance of a trot

XXXI

Town of Turtle Bay

Peterson found a mass grave behind the church atop a small hill. A few old men were slowly shoveling dirt onto dozens of corpses deep in the trench. A couple of old women knelt by the grave, faces drenched in tears, rosaries clenched in gnarled hands. Peterson walked up to one of the men.

"Cuántos?" he asked. The man just shrugged and went back to his work. He dropped a shovelful of dirt on a headless man in a priest's cassock and the wails of the women increased in volume. Peterson shook his head and turned away. As he made his way back down the hill, he noticed a man on a burro riding down the road into the other side of town. There was something very unpleasant about the man. Very unpleasant indeed. He turned and hurried back towards Janney. He could still see her a quarter mile away sitting in the front seat, long, bare, lovely legs sticking out of the open door. She had somehow changed into pink hot pants and a white diaphanous blouse with the top button undone. As he watched she raised one leg and braced it against a side mirror. He looked again at the man on the burro. Behind him were a couple of very nasty looking desperados. Janney didn't see them as she played with the radio. Peterson broke into a desperate run.

XXXII

Harbor of Turtle Bay

Janet and Jill were busy dropping the dinghy into the water alongside the 'Rose Marie', when Janet glanced aft and saw Larry holding her husband at knife point. With a shriek she charged aft and only stopped when he turned the knife and dug its blunt point into Harv's throat.

"You want your man alive, get all my money back into my bag, all of it, you hear? Get me food and water and a map and then take me ashore. I'm getting off this hell ship. All of you are totally crazy. I don't understand why you can't behave. I'm not the bad guy here. Do you hear? You were supposed to lie down and obey me.

"But, oh no, all of you have tied me up, poisoned me, stabbed me in the back, all this after I offered to pay for the trip. Really, it's like you all enjoy being a nuisance. I've had enough. If you want your life back, get me my stuff." Janet looked at him holding a knife to her husband's throat.

"Let Harv go, right now or we won't help you." He let go of the still comatose Harv, who then slid down onto the cockpit floor. "Look what you have done to my husband. He is dying, you bastard, you killed him."

"Yeah, you bastard pirate. Get off our boat. Bastard." Jill seemed to really like saying the word. She thought it made her sound salty. "Bastard, bastard, pirate."

Larry reached down, grabbed Harv's hair and pulled his head back exposing his throat. It seemed as if Harv took and extra deep breath but it was hard to be sure.   Janet looked at him quickly. She thought she saw his eyelids flutter.

"Money, water, map, food. If not, there won't be a question if your husband and father recovers. You can watch him die in front of you. Listen, if you like, I'll give you his head." He pulled Harv's head back even further and dug the knife deep into his neck.

"All right. OK. Relax. Jill, get the money. Put it in that valise. I'll get the food, water, and a map. You let go of my husband, now. Move, Jill, right now, I mean it."

Larry let go of Harv's hair and leaned back. He felt a little weak. Loss of blood he guessed. 'Not to worry,' he thought, 'I have always been a quick healer. I just have to get off this hell ship. These people are driving me crazy. Why can't they behave like normal people? Shit. These sailors deserve being stuck on these little boats in the middle of the fucking ocean.'

Jill was soon back with the money. He opened the bag and smiled. It was full of money. He touched it in reassurance. Freedom was a lot easier with money. Janet came back with a backpack of food and water with a topographical map sticking out of a side pocket.

"I'll row you ashore, Jill you stay here and care for your Dad. Let's go, tough guy." She dropped lightly into the dinghy and steadied it as he laboriously lowered himself down the side, trying not to open his back any further. He sat in silence as she stroked the oars. Soon they were alongside the dock next to a rusty ladder.

"Listen, no hard feelings, huh?" She ignored his thrust out hand, with a look of distaste on her face. A flare ignited deep in his eyes. He reached out and grabbed her neck hairs, pulled her head back and kissed her full on the mouth. She tried to bite him, but then, despite all her hatred of the man, despite all her worries about Harv, in spite of her stubborn spirit, despite knowing her daughter was on the boat watching her, she felt her back arch and her nipples harden. To her horror, she felt her legs start to open, and a hint of moisture forming there. She pushed him away with the last of her strength. Her muscles felt like putty. Her normally strong will dissolved around him. She didn't know what it was about this guy.

He seemed to be able to turn her on with such ease. It was like he wasn't even trying; like he was just playing with her because he had nothing else to do. And she hated it, hated it; really, really hated it.

"Goddamn you. Get off my boat. I hope I never see you again, you, you asshole. Get out, get out, get out. NOW."

He pulled himself up the ladder, at the top he turned, looked down at her, and smiled a little smile. And then he was gone.

XXXIII

Puebla of Turtle Bay

Raoul saw a white land rover parked on the side of the road in the middle of town, someone sat in the passenger side. He couldn't quite tell who it was behind the sun glazed windscreen. He wondered if it was his grey eyed beauty. As he got a little closer he saw a feminine foot sticking out the open door wedged against the side mirror. He was sure it was her. It had to be her. He wanted it to be her in the worse way. He wanted it to be her with one leg up on the door, opening herself just for him. Yes, she wanted him. From the corner of his eye he noticed a man rushing towards the car. Someone was trying to get to his girl, first.

"We will see about that, you stinking hombre. You stinking dead meat. Gomez." The big burly man with the scar ambled forward.

"Si, Jefe." Raoul pointed at the man rushing towards the range rover and made a sweeping motion to the left.

"Simone." The tall woman flashed forwards and knelt at Raoul's burro's hoofs.

"Si, Patron." He pointed at the man and then made a sweeping motion from the right.

"And now, my little grey eyed beauty," he murmured to himself, "while your boyfriend is otherwise occupied, we are going to get better acquainted." He threw back his head and laughed. He ignored a bit of saliva that dripped from the right corner of his mouth. It dribbled down through his long unkempt beard, made its way past a piece of yesterday's tortilla and fell to the ground.

Gomez and Simone circled around until they were on either side of Peterson. In front of Peterson was the range rover. He could see Janney relaxed inside with her eyes closed, enjoying the sun shining through the windscreen. Behind her a small man, maybe a midget, sat on a burro, drooling. He clicked open the safety on the shotgun and spread his legs, better able to move in any direction. Into this standoff strolled Volcano Williams. He took one look at the battle field from the top of a low hill and ducked behind a small tree or big shrub. He couldn't decide which. Thick enough to hide him.

"Damn it all, I get off a ship from hell and run into a cheap western," he whispered to himself. "And they all look like they are more than willing to kill a guy with a valise full of money." He looked closer at the land rover and at Janney inside. "Well, now, you don't look like a girl who would stab a good looking man in the back. In fact, I think you would love, absolutely love, to be saved. And I sure could use those wheels." He looked closely at her. She seemed familiar some how. Someone he had met before. He settled down to watch developments and think about the girl. The problem was he had used so many women in his life, they tended to blend together. He tried to think of any one woman that stood out from the others. He could remember the cities, kind of; he could remember the scores, oh, yeah, he could remember the jobs, especially the scams, in detail. But the women? He thought this one down the hill was fairly recent. The only woman who came to mind was Lucy. Damn, that was one hell of a broad. So much had happened after he had got on that stupid boat, it was hard to keep everything straight. He couldn't believe people voluntarily went to sea in those things. Unsafe at any time, any where, any how,' he thought with a laugh.

He watched as a cop looking man rushed towards the land rover only to be intercepted by a huge Mexican, biggest man he had ever seen and a thin rangy woman with stringy black hair and a machete in a scabbard tied to her leg. The two newcomers stood ten feet away on either side of the cop and waited, patiently. If the cop moved towards the car one or the other of the desperados would be behind him.

XXXIV

Town of Turtle Bay

Peterson didn't like how it was playing out. These two locals were trying to keep him from Janney and he didn't like it one bit. Not one bit at all.

"Stand aside. I am a United States Police Officer. I order you to stand aside." The two Mexicans didn't even react; they didn't even raise an eyebrow. It was like they had heard the same thing thousands of times before. The woman just kept staring at his crotch. Her left hand opening and squeezing shut, over and over.

Peterson turned and started backing up towards the car, keeping the giant and the woman in view. He raised his shotgun, cocked the hammer, and aimed it at the big man. A shot rang out from behind them. Peterson heard a bullet go whizzing past his head. He spun and looked at the little man besides the car. He had a pistol in his hand, but was ignoring everyone except Janney. When the shot rang out, for the first time the desperados looked worried. Peterson thought he heard something the woman said about the Jefe's eye not being in today. The big man just shook his head.

Peterson slowly walked towards the two, casually aiming the gun somewhere between the two of them. As he got closer the two of them separated. The woman eased over five feet to the right and pulled the machete from her scabbard while the big man sidled over to the left and stood one foot in front of the other and waited.

As he approached within a few feet equally distant between the two; the big man let out a howl and raced around him to the left. Peterson followed him with the gun but just in time realized how stupid that was. He dropped and rolled forward and away from the woman. He twisted and held up the gun with two hands, one on the stock and one on the barrel, to block the machete's blade singing towards his head. As the blade hit the barrel with a shower of sparks he kicked up under the gun and hit the woman right square in the belly. It was like he had kicked a locomotive. The shock reverberated down his leg and into his hands holding the gun. He almost dropped it. He kicked again with both feet and snaked backwards still on his back.

"Where is that fucking giant?" he wondered. He chanced a quick look at the Range Rover and saw the little man on the burro reaching for Janney. He let go a quick shot over the man's head, not wanting to take a chance of hitting Janney, and then quickly brought the gun back down and fired at the machete woman. He realized he was in this fight for his and Janney's life. The time for the niceties of civilization was gone. The woman jumped sideways as he fired and he missed.

Suddenly the gun disappeared from his hands. He had it, and then it was gone. The giant. He jumped to his feet and zigzagged behind a small adobe house as the giant fired the shotgun over and over at him. He heard Janney screaming in the car; screaming in a panic fueled voice.

He didn't have time for her. Unless he could better the odds they both were dead. He pulled the .357 out of his belt and took a quick look around the corner. The giant was admiring the shotgun running his hands along the barrel. He fired a quick shot at the giant. He was sure he hit him. The guy was so big it would be hard to miss. He steadied his aim for a better shot, right into the heart, and was about to squeeze the trigger when his head was pulled back by a rope around his neck. Someone's foot was in the middle of his back, his legs under him, his neck pulled back until he felt his spine was going to break. The machete hit his pistol hand with the back of the blade and he involuntarily dropped his gun. He rolled his eyes up and saw a face from hell, eyes wide and gleaming, framed by wild stringy black hair flying in all directions as she pulled her end of the rope with all her strength. It was the machete woman and it seemed she was intent on tearing him in half. His feet were under him and pinned by his weight. He could hear his spine making popping noises. His head and back were pulled so far back, he was sure the slightest movement would split his spine. Behind him he heard a low grunt and the foot was replaced by a sharp machete blade, pushed hard against his lower back. He felt the blade find the space between two of his vertebrae. He struggled for a split second, but the pain in his back became so intense. The voice behind him started to laugh. Then to giggle. Then it was silence. Silence save for the popping of his back and the blood dripping into the dirt from the machete tip stuck in his lower back. Dripping faster as the woman twisted the blade around, feeling for the spinal cord between his vertebra.

XXXV

Puebla of Turtle Bay

Raoul liked the girl better and better, as he neared the vehicle. She had her eyes closed and was listening to her iPod. Her fingers were strumming on her right leg that was propped out of the open window. He stopped the burro and stared, stunned at her pink hot pants. At her long, beautiful legs, spread open, just for him, he was sure. He was used to overdressed Mexican women and the fat, sexless women on boats and in RVs from El Norte. He had never seen someone like this. In movies, sure. But in life, never. What ever he did, he whispered to himself,

"I must be very careful not to get those pink pants dirty. Maybe I will start a new collection. How many eyes can a man own?" But pants? He could smell them. He could dress up women in them before the kill. He could relieve this moment all over again. He felt his tiny organ growing almost hard just looking at the pants.

He looked up to see how his crew were doing with hombre. The man looked like a tough guy. Maybe this girl liked tough men. He pulled out his pistol and snapped a shot at the man. He didn't bother to watch if his shot went home. He just glared at the woman to show how tough he was. Again his eyes were drawn towards the hot pants. He imagined his little organ was bigger than it had ever been.

"Ay, ya, ya. I have invented a new aphrodisiac. Who needs cactus buds that never work anyway?" The girl had looked up at the sound of his shot and was shivering in fear. Just the way he liked his women. On their knees, petrified from fear, mouths open, awed by his presence.

He kicked his burro into motion, he reached down into the open door of the car grabbed the woman's arm and urged the burro back, pulling her out of the car. Suddenly she was fighting, struggling, biting, hitting. He slung her over his saddle. Her fists were flying everywhere. He was puzzled what to do for a moment. He didn't want anything to happen to his magical pants. As she twisted around, fighting, he got a brief look at her face.

"And my last set of eyes will be yours my innocent one. What a way to end my collection." He didn't want to cut off her nose which he usually did to shut bitches up; she might get blood on his magic pants. Finally he hit her across the back of the head with the handle of his pistol. The woman groaned and collapsed across the saddle, butt up. He thought about spanking her, he thought about sticking his pistol deep between her legs, just for the fun of it, but he didn't want to get the hot pants, dirty.

Raoul finally looked up to find out how the girl's man had died and was shocked to see Gomez walking around with his hands over his belly, red blood flowing out between his fingers, a shocked look on a face slowly turning white. There was no sign of Simone or the man. He carefully edged his burro forward, twirling his pistol around his trigger finger.

"I am the only one allowed to kill my men. No stinking gringo is going to shoot Gomez without paying for it, goddamn it," he mumbled to himself. His donkey worked its way around a small house. Simone had the gringo twisted almost in half, a rope tied around his neck, led back to her waist, where she had tied it. Her machete was jabbed into the small of his back. A steady stream of blood was dripping out of his spine and into the dust. With her spare hand she was shaving the hair from his scalp with a small knife. A few places she missed and gouged out sections of skin.

"Let him go, Simone. I want him to suffer for his sin. I want him to suffer for hours. I want to hear him scream, to cry like a baby, to beg to be killed. I want this one," he motioned at the unconscious woman across his saddle, "to beg for his life. I want this one to cut off her own fingers to save the man's life. Not that she will." He laughed a terrible, crazed, insane laugh.

145

XXXVI

A Hill overlooking Turtle Bay

As Simone let Peterson go with a last brutal jab, Larry looked up at the sound of the insane laugh that carried over the town like a bugle call. A call that alerted all in the vicinity that something was happening. He had been cleaning his fingernails with a cactus spine as the woman and the giant had attacked the cop. He didn't care who won. He had no use for cops and he hated gang members. He liked to pull a heist and then split. Less chance for informants that way. He liked to work alone. The fewer people to rat to the cops. He sometimes liked to work with women. They were easy to scare. Easy to convince that he would come back and cut their face if they talked. Not that he would, but as long as they believed it. He tried to remember all the women and all of his crimes for the last seven years. The crimes he could still be tried for. Thanks to the Statute of Limitations. There were so many, and so many girls, so many possible informants. Maybe he should just stay out of the country for a while.

As he heard a crazed laugh he looked up from his hands and saw the little guy on the donkey with the girl from the car face down across his saddle and lap. Her cute ass framed in pink shorts looked familiar but he had seen so many butts over the years it was difficult to decide if he knew this one. It was something to think about as they killed each other off and left him the car. He was patient; he was used to being patient. You can't do time unless you are patient. He opened his valise while waiting and decided to count his money. He pulled out the first bunch of bills and played with them a bit then looked down into the hole in the money he had formed. It was nothing but paper! His money was gone! Someone had taken his money and replaced it with worthless paper with just a bit of real money on top. It must have been that rotten little girl; he was starting to regret he had ever saved her from the weirdo rapist in the first place. That girl was nothing but trouble. He hadn't ever really decided to help her in the first place, anyway. Something had just come over him. Oh, yeah. The weirdo. Well, he had always hated weirdos. It was just so easy to get in trouble in this great big confusing world. Better just to stick with what you know. Like stick ups. Like women. And the hell if he ever got on a stupid boat again.

He looked out onto the harbor. The boat was still there. The little girl was now out in the dinghy rowing around the boat. It didn't look like they were going anywhere soon. He looked back at the car. That came first. Who ever won might drive away in the car. The boat would stay where it was until the man recovered or died. Whatever. He saw some small rowing boats along the beach. He could always get out to the sailboat. It wasn't like they were going to spend all his money sitting in a harbor. Their time was coming. Can't let people steal from him whenever they wanted to, you get a bad reputation that way. Someone would tell someone else, who would tell someone else. Soon everyone would know he was an easy touch.

And then what? People would start ordering him around, spitting in his face, and then cry when he pushed them. That's what happens when you lose your street cred. Well, it wasn't going to happen to him. It damn well wasn't going to happen to him. Didn't matter who got hurt. A guy has to look out for number one. Especially against rotten little girls, who needed to be taught a lesson.

XXXVII

Harbor of Turtle Bay

Jill was screaming at the top of her voice as she rowed around and around the Rose Marie in her little rowing dinghy.

"All right! At last, something is going right! The pirate is gone and Sir Daddy has woken up. The pirate is gone! The pirate is gone! We won!"

Janet looked at her in amusement from the cockpit as she cuddled her husband's head in her lap. She ran her fingers through his hair as he looked up at her adoringly.

"A guy like me, I am so lucky to have a gal like you. One that fights off pirates, sails the boat, finds the right port, and saves the day. What a lucky guy I am!"

"Hey! I'm the one who speared him like a big fat grouper! Don't forget how lucky you are to have me, too! Ole Dead Eye Jill! Yep. I saved the day again." Under her breath she added, "And made us a pile of money."

"Jill, you are a wonderful girl, the best there ever was. Now will you please land your dinghy and get me some bandages for your daddy's poor hand?"

Harv held the hand in his lap and tried not to look at it. It had swollen and turned blue and now was slowly becoming black. It no longer even looked human. More like something a monster from outer space might have hanging from a tentacle. Janet massaged it as gently as she could. She tried to ease the bones back into their sockets; to soothe damaged tendons and tortured muscles. Harv tried to ignore the pain of having his hand touched as well as he could, but he couldn't avoid wincing on occasion and once couldn't bite back a gasp as Janet pushed his thumb back into place. The pain was so indescribable, he preferred to watch his daughter, risen from the grave, row about the boat in ultimate happiness. It had turned out alright. Maybe he hadn't played the most important role in the victory, but he had done the best he could. And you can't ask more of that from any man.

"I don't think anything is broken, Honey. But you have seriously dislocated it."

"Daddy! Sir Daddy! Look at me! Come on, look at me!" Harv raised his head and saw his daughter standing in the dinghy with an oar over her head swinging it around for who knows what reason.

"Jillian, get back here right now. Stop playing around. Your father needs you. Try to act your age. I need some bandages. Do you want your father to bleed to death while you are playing swashbuckler?" Jill rowed back to the boat and tied off her dinghy with a well practiced bowline. With a leap she was in the cockpit.

"Honey, I know this hurts. But we don't have the money to fly you back to the states for proper medical care. Besides, fly from where." She looked around and saw only a beautiful harbor, half fronted by a seedy Mexican town. "Hold your breath, I only have a few big bones to move back into place." As Harv started to scream, finally, from the indescribable pain, Jill put a hand out and across her mother's arm.

"Mom, we have lots of money. I didn't give it all back to

the pirate. I just put a few bills on top of all my monopoly money and a lot of ripped up algebra homework that I was supposed to do over. But Mom, we have thousands. No, we have over a hundred and fifty thousand dollars! Mom, were rich!" Janet's eyes glowed for a second, but then a shadow came over them.

"Jill, what if he comes back. Jill, if he finds out and I am sure he will, he will come back and I can't even imagine what he might do to us. Look what he did to poor Harv already. Oh, Jill, I'm so worried."

"Mom, we are way out here in the bay. How is he going to get out here? We have the dinghy. He can call and call for us to came ashore and pick him up. I'm the official dinghy rower and I'm not going to pick up some rotten pirate, so there.

"Anyway, I just saved the day, again. Why aren't you thanking me? We can get Dad fixed up. We can buy Dad his anchor winch he always wanted. We can go out to breakfast every morning, for like, forever, if we want to. We can get triple candy at the movies. This is going to be so much fun!"

Janet turned her worried eyes towards the town. She heard the sound of a shotgun blast.

XXXVIII

Puebla of Turtle Bay

Raoul rode his burro over to where Gomez was rocking on his knees in the dust holding his belly with both hands. Beside him in the dust was Peterson's shotgun. Blood was running down his pants and into the dust forming a small red pool.

"Hand me the gun, you stupid Mexican, before you get it all bloody. What are you doing on your knees, anyway? I thought you were one tough dude, you silly little, tiny man." Gomez managed to hand up the shotgun holding it by the barrel. The stock of the weapon touched Janney smearing some dust across her thigh. Raoul's eyes widened and his blood pressure rose alarmingly streaking his eyes pulsating red lines.

"You have ruined my collection, you, you peon. You got them dirty, dirty, dirty! Idiot!"

Raoul grabbed the gun slipping his finger inside the trigger guard and fired a solid slug right into Gomez's chest. He ratcheted the weapon and fired a buckshot shell and blew Gomez's head right off in a flurry of blood and bone. The burro gave a little side step that almost unseated Raoul. He leaped from the saddle and blew off the animal's head also. The burro fell to the ground tossing Janney to the side as it fell.

"I like this gun. And I like my new car. It is time I moved up in the world. Time to get out of this stinking desert, with stinking burros and stinking idiot gangs, and head back to Mexico City. They thought they could run me out? Ha, I run them out, amigo," he told the dead Gomez. The whites of his eyes were almost entirely red from rage.

Simone was staring at Raoul. As he turned his little pig eyes on her she quickly averted her gaze and gave Peterson a vicious kick in the short ribs. She smiled as she felt one of them snap.

"Jefe, what about him? Do I get him, Senor?"

"Tie him to a tree, get all his money and his credit cards. And wake up that bitch, she is getting dirt on my pants." He thought about striping the pants off of her before she could dirty them, but he wanted to see her die in them, to see her shake and shiver in pain, to see her twist and turn as she tried to get away. To see the pants quiver and shake as she suffered.

"Tie her to the front of my new car. Spread eagle her across the hood, tie her so her head hangs down by the radiator grill. Tie her so she can watch her man die, upside down."

Simone's eyes glinted in the sunlight and she licked her lips as she pulled some line out of the saddlebags on the dead burro. She quickly stripped Janney's blouse and bra off and tied her feet to the side view mirrors, her hands stretched out sideways towards the ends of the fenders. Peterson, she tied to an old, mostly dead tree.

Raoul had been going through the girl's purse and had all of her credit cards laid out on the hood of the car. He found a piece of paper and a pencil. On the other side of the hood Simone had all of Peterson's credit and bank cards lined up.

"We are ready, Jefe."

"Wake them up first, Simone. I want them to enjoy their deaths!" He slid into the driver's seat, started the motor and drove towards the tree till Janney's head and Peterson's crotch were only 3 feet away.

"Now we see which one will break first. This will be muy fun!" he giggled.

XXXIX

Hill overlooking Turtle Bay

Larry heard the car start while stretched under the tree where he had been resting. He felt good, much better. His nap had helped his wound. He felt his back with his hand. It had stopped bleeding. With a careful twist he raised his head to see what they were doing with his vehicle. They had the girl tied to the hood of his car and were shouting that they were going to break her neck against the guy tied to the tree if he didn't tell them the security codes for his credit cards. They inched his car closer and closer to the tree. Her head was going to hit the guy's crotch first.

Larry laid down again and closed his eyes. Looked like it was going to be the Mexicans he would have to deal with later. He didn't care. He could use some more sleep as they played games. Besides, the winner's edge would be off when they won. He wouldn't even have to kill anyone. Just waltz in, bash 'em about a bit, take his car, get his money back from the stupid kid, and take off. Life was so good.

He wondered if he should go to Costa Rica or Belize. He had heard good things about both. Costa Rica was prettier and more modern, but still, you could live the life of ease in Belize with no extradition treaty with the USA. Whatever, he was sure both of them had big stores and maybe banks to rob when he became bored with his retirement. He normally didn't like banks. They had far too much security. He thought about the cameras, exploding money filled with dye, guards with guns, homing devices. No banks weren't worth it. They were just too well defended. Fuck banks, especially when they left money laying around stores just begging someone to take it. They didn't have to beg him twice, and that's the fucking truth.

He shut his eyes, ignored the screams from down by the car and dozed off. He wondered if they had women in Costa Rica like Lucy. That sure was one hot chick. The way her eyes shown, the way she flipped her hair back when she wanted to be noticed. One hot gal. He thought about her up on that counter top, eyes flaring. No doubt about it. One damn hot chick. And he fell back asleep.

XL

Port of Turtle Bay

Harv sat up a little straighter. He was sure he heard screaming.

"Honey. Janet? Sweetheart? Where are you?" He looked wildly about. Janet stuck her head up from the cabin where she had been looking for bandages. "Oh, there you are. Do you hear any screaming coming from shore? I'm sure I heard something. Wait. There, there it is again. Did you hear it? Someone is in trouble. A lot of trouble. I have to go and help them."

"You aren't going anywhere. You are one sick puppy and you are in no condition to rush around playing Sir Galahad. Just lay back down and rest, baby. You have done enough."

"Janet, people are in trouble. I can't just lay here. I have to try to help. Look I know I can't do much with only one hand. But I am feeling better already. Look, I think I moved a finger. Look!" He held up a mangled hand. There was no movement at all in any of the fingers. The hand did look better, more like a hand, but it was all black now, as black as death.

"Anyway, it doesn't matter. I can't stay hear and listen to

them scream, I just can't. It would drive me insane."

Janet remembered how he had come to her aid when her apartment was burgled and no one else would help. It was one of the things she loved about him. She decided she was going to have to help him, help others. He was such a great guy. Besides if he went by himself he might get killed. If she went with him she could keep him out of trouble, keep him safe. She could keep him away from who ever was screaming and who ever was making them scream. She could row real slow, take her time. Draw things out. Maybe it would be all over by the time they arrived. She wondered if she was a monster, not caring about other people. But they were strangers. Her man wanted to do the right thing, because he was a good man. It was up to her to save him from himself. She might be a monster, but she was a monster who loved her man.

"Alright, Honey. If it means so much to you I'll row you ashore and help you find those people."

"I am so coming too! You betcha! Are we ever going to get that pirate. We'll show him a thing or two. Anyone that comes up against our family will learn the facts of life. And that's the truth! And, I'll pack us a picnic in case we get hungry! Fighting pirates is hungry work. I'll bring us something to drink, too!"

"Baby, you are going to stay right here and lock yourself down below. You are not coming ashore. Besides, Larry is long gone, I am sure. A harbor like this is no place for a young lady like yourself. That is an order, Jill!"

"Jill, your Mother is right. Besides, if you come ashore no one will be here to protect the boat. What if that pirate comes back for his booty? He could jump on board, take it, and be gone before anyone knew it. Yes, your duty is to stay here. OK?"

Jill looked stubbornly at her father who stared sternly back at her. They dueled with stares for a few minutes until Jill looked down first.

"Alright, Dad. I'll stay and protect the booty, if you want me to. But I think you guys are hogging all the fun and it is not fair. It isn't fair, is it, Sir Daddy?"

"Life isn't fair, pumpkin. That is one of the hardest things to learn growing up." He looked down at his hand. "Life isn't fair at all."

XLI

Pueblo of Turtle Bay

Raoul inched the car closer to the tree till the girl's head was jammed up against the man's crotch. Still, he motored slowly closer. He could hear her neck start to make stretching noises. Slowly he reversed a touch.

"The numbers, Senora, the codes for the cards. What are they?" He held up a Visa card. "Tell me the security code for this one, Senora," he asked in an almost gentle sing song voice. "The gold Visa one, Senora."

Some muffled words came out of her mouth. He backed up the car a touch more.

"Fuck you."

"Puta," he screamed at her. "The code, give me the code." He slammed his fist down on her right breast, flattening it. Janney's back arched in agony. A moan of intense pain escaped thru her gritted teeth.

"Yo, hombre! Yes, you, asshole. You, copper. Do you want me to kill this woman in front of you. I'll cut her, I'll cut her bad, hombre." Simone lay her machete on the side of her left breast, the cutting edge just touching where it rose from her chest.

"Here are your cards. Tell me the codes or she loses a tit. Tell me, hombre, tell me now!" Simone started a slight sawing motion with her blade just touching the side of the breast. A few drops of blood ran down her side and dripped onto the hood of the car.

"OK. OK. OK. Stop cutting her. I'll tell you, I'll tell you." Simone just smiled at him and continued cutting, her nostrils flaring as the blood ran down and cooked on the hot hood. She pinched the nipple between two fingers and pulled it up to see what damage she had done. She smiled to find that she had cut a noticeable slice. She looked down at the screaming bitch tied to the car.

"Shut up, senora. Or I will give you something to scream about." She lowered the blade of her machete to Janney's upside down nose and started to cut the soft tissues between the nostrils.

"I'll talk, I'll tell you. Just get that bitch away from

Janney. Get her away," Peterson screamed, struggling against his bonds.

Raoul picked up his piece of paper and pencil again and waited expectantly. With a sob, Peterson gave codes, credit rating, numbers, banks; he told everything he knew.

"Bueno. And now, Senora. Give me your numbers." Janney shook her head, no. She was sure they were going to kill them anyway. Why should they profit from her death? That would just encourage them to kill others in the same way.

"Simone, convince her," Raoul ordered. Simone cut the pants off of Peterson with a single well practiced motion. She forced his clothes down past her face. She wedged the blade of the machete under his manhood and started sawing inches from her face. Blood was soon running down his legs and splattering into her eyes.

"Janney, Janney! Tell them. They are going to cut it off. They are going to cut all of it off! Tell them, honey. I told for you. Save me, Janney! Save me!"

"No! No, no, no. Never. Get me away from his body! Get me away from it!" Simone shoved his manhood into her mouth, and started slicing just in front of her lips.

"Better talk, Senora. Or after it is cut off, you are going to eat it."

XLII

Port of Turtle Bay

Janet and Harv landed on the pebble beach, tied off the dinghy to a small tree and climbed the hill. Janet stopped every ten feet to adjust her shoelaces or her backpack. Finally on the top they looked down the other side to a scene from Hades. Two people were torturing two others, one tied atop a car and the other tied to a tree. Before Janet could say anything, before she could move, Harv was shouting and running down the hill.

"Hey, let go of them! You there! Stop it. What you are doing is wrong, dead wrong. Leave them alone. Stop it, I said." His bad hand flopped at his side as he ran down the hill.

The guy by the car started to smile and got a gun out of the front seat, he balanced it on the top of the car roof. He squeezed the trigger just as Harv tripped on a rock and started tumbling down the hill.

A cross look passed over Raoul's face and he aimed the gun again. Janet jumped up and down on the side of the hill trying to distract the shooter.

"Hey, up here, dumb fuck. What are you worried about him for? You want action? Come and get it. I'll wait right here, asshole." Janet ducked behind a bush as the gun pointed in her direction and then fell to the ground as a bullet came whizzing through the bushes. She rolled over on her back, tears of worry in her eyes. She hoped Harv would understand that she was doing this for him.

"Hey big shot! I'm up here on my back with my legs open; why don't you come up and get some! Unless you are too scared. You scared little boy." She couldn't believe such filth was coming out of her mouth. But she didn't know what else she could do. Poor Harv. He didn't stand a chance against those killers. The pirate was bad enough. But all he wanted was money. These, these desperados were killing just for the fun of it.

With an oath, Raoul backed the Land Rover away from the tree and raced it up the hill, crashing and bumping through pot holes and over the boulders. Credit cards, ignored, went flying every which way. Janney, still tied to the hood, bounced up and down with the car, coming down hard on her spine each time. She tried to twist her spread legs to protect her lower back but it was no use. Her head crashed down on the radiator grill on each bounce wrenching her neck. Blood seeped out of her mouth where she had bitten her tongue. Blood still leaked out from the cut between her nostrils and into her nose. As it filled her sinuses she sneezed it out in big bursts.

When Janet saw the car coming, she ran down the far side of the hill as fast as she could; weaving around small bushes and rocks. She could hear him cursing at the wheel and a woman screaming behind her. Boulders were everywhere. She leapt from one to another praying she wouldn't trip, praying they wouldn't catch her. Harv was the hero, not her! She didn't want to be tied on top of some car!

Harv put his shoulders back and marched up to where the man was tied to the tree. The Mexican woman with short hair and a busted nose just stood and watched him. As he started to untie the ropes one handed, she walked around the tree and stared at his hand.

"You want me to cut that off for you?' She asked indicating the busted hand.

"You mean the ropes? Sure, cut the ropes, if you don't mind. It would really help." She flashed her machete down between his belt and his back and cut his belt and the top of his pants off. As his pants fell down, she spun him with a wiry hand, talon like fingers dug into his shoulder and threw him to the ground. He was wearing no underwear.

"Ay, ya. You have a big one. I think I should cut it off. Save the poor senoritas in the world from being enslaved by your thing. You want me to do that, little man?"

"You have no right to treat people like this. It is wrong. I don't like your behavior when you act like this. I want you to act like the good person you are, deep inside. I know you are rough and tough. I know you have to be; for someone like yourself who has been treated so poorly by men. Men have done bad things to you haven't they?"

"Hey, Gringo. You want to see me treat you badly? Huh? I show you bad. I like being bad, you white puta." She reached down and flipped his organ back and forth with the tip of her machete.

"What the fuck is the matter with this thing? You can't get it up? Huh? You fucking white college boy with all the big words? I'm going to have to think of something special to do to you. Something muy painful that will teach you about being treated; what did you say? Si, I will teach you about being treated poorly. You will learn, you dumb fuck. Or you will die. Maybe you die anyway, only God knows."

She turned as Janet came running around the hill straight for her. She stepped away from Harv and raised her machete as Janet charged at her, arms pumping, mouth snarling, eyes glaring. Ten feet away she skidded to a stop.

"Get away from my husband, you, you tramp."

Just behind her, roared the land rover, still bumping over the rough terrain. Janney was now screaming, yelling, sneezing blood out every few seconds.

"Stop this stupid car. Stop it now! You are killing me, you bastard. Do you hear me, are you deaf? Stop this car!"

Raoul wasn't paying any attention to Janney. He had forgotten about the grey eyes and the hot pants. The only thing he cared about now was that vixen he was chasing that he couldn't seem to catch.

"Don't killer her, Simone. Don't kill her. I want to do it. I want to do it so bad. She has to be taught to respect men. She has to learn that, if it is the last thing she ever learns, the puta."

Glaring at Simone, Janet walked forward staring at her in the eyes. She grabbed Harv's good hand and pulled him to his feet with a grunt. She gave him a shove in the back.

"Run, Harv. Make them chase you. Run!" Harv gave her a worried look and took off running holding the remains of his pants up around his waist with his good hand. Simone ignored him. She slid sideways to keep Janet between her and the approaching range rover. Janet took off to the left, away from Harv, struggling over the cactus and rocks off the road. Simone kept up with her easily, loping across the rough terrain as easily as a wolf.

"Give up, Senora. He is going to have you one way or the other. You are just making it hard on yourself. Chances are you will trip over something and bash all your teeth in. There is no dignity in dying with all your teeth broke off."

Janet ignored her and continued as fast as she could. Off to her left she saw the car had flanked her and was going to cut her off just ahead. She stopped and raced back the way she had come. She tried to keep out of range as she passed Simone. It was no good though. Simone's machete flashed out and hit Janet on the back of the head, and laid her out cold.

Harv saw Janet go down and raced to her side, yelling, screaming. Raoul snapped off a shot, and Harv went down.

"Finally, I got my eye back in. 'Bout fucking time."

"Si, Jefe."

XLIII

Hilltop of Turtle Bay

Larry sat on top of his hill watching the show with a smile on his face, his head swirling as he watched all the action circling around him. At times he giggled to himself.

"This is better than TV," he laughed. "And, now what is this? Damn, I need some popcorn."

Below him, across the harbor, Jill was paddling ashore on her boogie board, a slingshot stuck in her back pocket, a determined look on her face. She was making good progress, Larry guessed, and should arrive at the beach in another 10 minutes. It was like having your own play. Put on just for you. He watched as Jill made it to the beach. He saw her dig a hole just above the high water mark and bury a plastic bag inside of it. She rolled a big rock over the hole, to mark it, and started up the side of the hill. Larry settled down against a sun warmed boulder and watched the proceedings with a satisfied look on his face. Life was so fucking good.

XLIV

Pueblo of Turtle Bay

"Bueno, Simone. Good job. And now we tie them all up and have some fun, especially with this one. This one, she will take a long time to die. This one, we will remember." Suddenly, Harv was back on his feet. He had tripped just as Raoul's bullet passed over his head.

"Get away from my Janet, you, you bastards. Get away." Harv ran up to Raoul who was prodding Janet's left breast with the toe of his boot, as if to tell if it was done yet. Harv tried to tackle Raoul with a flying dive, but Raoul sidestepped at the last moment with out even looking at Harv, who ended up skidding face down into the dirt and rocks.

"And this one too, tie them all up. This one with the hand, tie his feet to the tree and his hands, OK, hand, to the bumper of the car and we will back up and see which gets torn off first. We let my grey eyed beauty see all of it. I want her eyes to be full of fear when I tear them out. This one," he pointed to Janet, "the one with the mouth, tie one foot to the tree and the other foot to the car. We will see if she likes her legs spread. We will see."

"Where the fuck are my credit cards?" He rushed over to the hood of the range rover and ran his hands over the hood. "Where the hell are my credit cards? Some one is going to pay for this. Someone is going to pay for this with agony."

Simone dragged the 180 pound Harv over to the tree seemingly without effort and tied his feet to the tree, just below Peterson's knees. Next to him, she tied the still unconscious Janet. They would be able to look into each others eyes as they saw each other's bodies ripped apart.

"I am an American Police officer. I demand that you stop what you are doing, release us and stand against the car with your hands behind your heads. I am the law. Do what I say. What you are doing is inhumane, it is vile, it is animal, worse than animal, worse than criminal. It is something I would only expect in the deepest dungeons of hell. That is where you belong. Hell! Go! May merciful Jesus send an angel of death to send you there, you, you, you toys of the devil."

Simone looked over at Raoul. He nodded his head, ever so slightly, with a crooked smile in his eyes. Simone pulled her machete out of its scabbard that was tied to her upper thigh and walked over to the tree. She stood square in front of Peterson, legs apart, balanced on her toes, machete held in both hands stretched above her head. She looked at Peterson straight in the eyes as he continued to shout, 'angel of death,' and brought the heavy blade down in a surging swoop hitting the very top of his head. The razor sharp machete cut down and through his skull, between his eyes, cutting his nose in half, knocking out teeth as it split his jaws and down through his neck. The two sides of his head fell apart sideways, exposing the perfectly split halves of his brain. One eye lay next to each shoulder, a half a tongue stuck out of each half mouth.

Raoul held Janney's head towards Peterson and kept her eyes open with his thumbs dug in above her eyes and into the upper sockets. Janney couldn't help herself. She threw up in a surge. Yellow stinking spew went down her nose and out into Peterson's remains. Thankfully it ran into her eyes, hiding the horror from her view.

XLV

Port of Turtle Bay

Jill crawled Indian style down the hill until she was in range of the tree and car. Two people were trying to wake up the lady on top of the car. They were slapping her face and the man pored beer down her nose, which made the lady snort and sneeze and wake up. The little man got into the car and slowly started to back up. He mother and father were tied between the car and the tree. Jill had loaded up with pebbles from the beach. Pulling out her trusty slingshot she fired into the window of the car and nailed the little man right in the ear with a big pebble.

Jill giggled to herself as the man looked around wildly. She fired again and got a lucky shot right on his nose. She rolled over behind a bush and listened to the man screaming in Spanish. After a few seconds, she rolled over to the other side of the bush and fired a perfectly round rock, her best one. It hit the man right in the teeth. Jill was sure she heard one crack. As she started to load another she was suddenly lifted up into the air by an incredibly strong hand around the back of her neck.

"I have her, Jefe. It is a nina, Senor."

Raoul held a hand to his aching mouth. He felt blood seeping down his throat. His blood! Someone was going to die for this. Everyone was going to die for this.

"Bring her here, Simone. Bring her to me. Now."

"But, Jefe, she is only a nina. She was just playing. She won't bother us again. I promise, Senor."

"I said, bring her. Bring her now, you stupid bitch. Do you want to end up like Gomez? You think I can't take you, bitch? Bring her! Now, I said!" Slowly Simone carried the struggling, twisting, biting Jill over to Raoul.

"Forgive me, Nina." Simone whispered to Jill. "May the Virgin Mother take you quickly. Die easily, my little one. Don't fight it. Don't fight, Nina; just die and go to God. Life is much easier in heaven. Go with a smile, little one."

"Give her to me." Raoul looked down at the little girl. She was so small. She would make his small manhood feel big. And she liked to struggle. Good. That would make it more exciting.

"Simone, make sure no one escapes. I will be in that building over there. Remember, what I said. I can take you easy. Bang, one shot. And you are dead."

"Si, Jefe." He dragged the girl over to the building with one hand twisted in her hair. Soon screams and groans echoed out of the small building.

XLVI

Hillside of Turtle Bay

Larry woke up from a doze. He heard a girl screaming and yelling down the hill in the town. He thought for a minute, it sounded like that stupid girl from the boat. The one that stole his money. Good. He hoped she suffered. Damn, thieves. Suddenly the girl broke loose and ran out of the building, half naked. The man was soon after her. One of his fingers was bleeding from a bite which he was sucking on. He quickly caught her and hit her across the face with a closed fist. He grabbed a hand full of hair and pulled her into the air. With his other hand he smashed his fist straight into her face, breaking her nose.

Larry's eyes turned cold. Dead cold. His nostrils flared. The whites of his eyes shown all around his pupils. With an oath, his injured back forgotten, he straightened his arms, the ends of his fingers flickered straight, flinging him to his feet.

He walked down to the town. Walking easily, building up his energy, storing his fury, feeling it fill his muscles, his bones, his being. It seemed as if he had no weight. Only his toes touched the ground, so powerful was the spring in his step.

Simone backed away from him, bringing her machete up into a ready, defensive position as Larry's black on black eyes flicked like lightning in her direction. She took one look at his eyes and the way he walked, the way he soared, and backed up further.

Raoul felt him approach as he dragged the unconscious girl back to the house with a hand wrapped in her hair. He dropped Jill and drew his pistol and fired all in one smooth motion. He smiled. His eye was in. He could feel it. But the man was gone. He looked wildly around, backing up. Suddenly, there he was. A little to the right and closer than he was before. Just standing there, relaxed. As he watched, the man smiled. A nice smile, but he noticed that the eyes were not smiling at all. They were as hard as nails. Raoul fired again. It felt so good. He knew he had scored a hit. But the man was still standing there with the same stupid smile on his face. He had moved a little. Just enough to let the bullet go by.

"Hey, wetback," The man jeered at him from 30 feet to the left. Raoul told himself he was going to watch very carefully when he shot again. He wanted to know how that ghost was avoiding his bullets. "Hey wetback. Do you want to shoot me?" yelled the ghost.

Raoul turned and lined up his pistol. The guy was just staring straight into his eyes. Like he was hypnotizing him or something. As he slowly and carefully eased off a round he felt himself involuntarily jerk his pistol and missed wide to the right. He tried again and this time he felt his hand jerk to the left. The ghost just stood there and smiled a little smile at him. A stupid little smile. Foam lined Raoul's lips and in his anger his left pupil became smaller than his right. He emptied the pistol at the ghost firing wildly. Each bullet went flying off the mark. "Simone. Come. Get him." Simone looked at the little abused girl, her flat immature breasts scorched from a burning cigarette, laying and bleeding in the dust at Raoul's feet and drifted behind the tree.

"Simone, Simone. I said he is yours. You can do anything you want to him. Anything. Anything!" There was no response from the tree.

"Hey, stupid, wetback." Again Raoul spun and fired again. The gun clicked empty. The man stood up and walked towards him. Quickly he dropped the gun and slid out his machete.

"So you want to dance, ghost. Let's see if you can run from sharpened steel. Come on, punk, let's dance." Raoul's face was filled with anger. So much anger that it almost hid his underlying fear.

Larry walked up to Raoul, seemingly relaxed, but every muscle quivering ever so slightly with energy. He was about five feet away, well within the striking distance of the machete, even swung by such a small man. He would have to watch out for his knees.

"So stupido, what are you going to do, cut my toes?"

"Die, ghost, die." Screaming Raoul charged flinging his blade in every different direction in front of him. He knew the ghost would move, but he didn't know where or when.

But the ghost didn't move. As Raoul's right arm swung the blade, Larry twirled in the opposite direction, pulling his stomach in as the blade passed, he grabbed Raoul's upper arm as the machete almost ended its swing, used the force Raoul had put into the blow, and forced the midget's shoulder to follow the machete. Larry twisted to the ground, still spinning, Raoul's arm still held in his hands. As Raoul hit the ground, Larry's spin took him across Raoul's back and to his other side. He felt the arm dislocate. He continued his roll and tore Raoul's arm right off at the shoulder.

Raoul grabbed Larry's foot with his left hand and started to bite his Achilles' tendon. Larry kicked out with his other foot and hit the soft spot just above and in front of the ear. It would have killed a normal man. Raoul tossed it off with a shake of his head. He gathered all the anger and pain and torture of a wicked life and drove right at Volcano Adams. Larry dropped down on one knee and drove a fist right into Raoul's Adam's apple, paralyzing his throat.

Raoul dropped as if he was dead. His hands tore at his neck trying to find the reason he couldn't breathe. His face turned red then purple as he slowly suffocated. Realizing he was going to die, he charged once again at the ghost. He charged with every ounce of his being, with every memory of evil he had done, with every intention of doing it again. He charged snarling, eyes narrowed in hatred, mouth agape, teeth ready to slice and rip and tear, fingers curled, his back, twisted in anger. Blood ignored, it flowed in spurts from the socket his arm had been in. Larry dropped to one knee and sent every bit of his power to his right hand, to his open right hand. He envisioned his whole being, his whole soul flooding into his right hand. He jabbed out, fingers curled back, away from danger, the base of his palm forward, jabbed straight at Raoul's nose. The force, the ki, the aura, the whatever the fuck you want to call it, surrounding Larry's palm forced Raoul's head back before his hand even made contact. Larry's palm, when it landed, shot the cartilage of Raoul's nose deep into his brain killing him instantly.

Larry rose from the dust, turned and raised his head, from the corner of his eyes he saw Simone who was off to one side. He slowly turned his head, never moving his eyes till he was looking at her face on. She was terrified. She knew, she just knew, if she ran he would be on her in an instant. If she stayed he would kill her. She made a mistake. She raced to the range rover, tore open the door, and started the car with the keys that were still in the ignition.

As she reached to put it into gear, she was ripped from the car by a force greater than lightning and thrown against the trunk of the dead tree. Her back felt like it was broken but with a groan she forced herself to her feet and faced the Volcano. He walked slowly towards her, toying with the idea that he would let her go, being as she was a woman and all. His eyes strayed to the split head of Peterson, and mercy died in his soul. He stared deep into her eyes, reached out with a claw of a hand towards her left breast, a low animal snarl reverberated deep with in him, it grew in intensity, louder and louder, louder until it was a physical force emanating from him. His hand, three feet from Simone's breast closed around something and twisted 270 degrees and tore back as the sound from Larry's mouth attained a mind shattering angry banshee. Simone, her heart severed from its arteries, fell to her knees and then her face thudded into the dust and was still.

Larry untied the girl on the hood of his car. He hoped she hadn't scratched the damn paint. The one thing he hated was stealing a car that wasn't perfect. After all, if caught, you served the same amount of time for stealing a Jaguar as a junker. To his surprise, when she opened her eyes she seemed to recognize him.

"Volcano? Is that you? Oh, God, how I prayed you would save me! Thank you so much, so, so, so much!"

"That's not any Volcano. That is a pirate named Larry. He pirated our boat. Don't trust anything he says. Bastard." Her words were hard to understand thru her broken nose and her dazed demeanor. As Jill untied her mother and father, Janet looked at her sternly.

"Jill, your pirate just saved our lives. I think you owe him an apology. We would all be dead if it were not for Mr. Larry Adams."

"What? No. You are wrong. This is Volcano Williams. I know it is. I met him up north, just before I met," her eyes wandered to the tree where Peterson's body was still tied. "Before I met," she fell into tears, holding her face in her hands, peeking once between her fingers at the vomit covered corpse.

Larry ignored her and walked over to the tree and cut Peterson's body down. He looked around at the grisly scene. He felt like walking away from the whole mess, jumping in his car, and taking off. But the little girl was staring right at him, with an expectant look in her eyes.

"Fuck it," he thought. "I sure as hell ain't digging no fucking graves. That is not in the damn job description." He looked around the dusty town. He nodded slightly to himself once.

"Harv. Pick up an arm." Larry grabbed the other arm and motioned Janet to get the legs. He guided them over to a barely standing one room shack. They laid the body inside and Janney who had helped Janet with the other leg stayed inside to say a few words. She knelt for a few moments not looking at the head and then came out. Larry pushed against a barely standing wall and then jumped back as it collapsed over the body burying it entirely.

XLVII

Turtle Bay

"What did you bury on the beach?" Larry asked looking straight at Jill. "Don't lie. I saw you. Fess up."

"Girls never lie. Sometimes they just have to get creative to protect those less talented than themselves, like the entire male race. And it is a good thing you men have us around. What ever would happen to you if you didn't have us women to take care of you? So there. Besides, no one saw me on the beach. I made sure no one was watching me. You're just trying to trick me into telling you where my money is. You poor men could never trick a real woman. So there, bastard."

"Jill, go and get Mr. Adams' money right now." Her father gave her a stern look. "All of it this time Jill. All of it." Jill gave her father a stubborn look. "Jill, you have no idea what would have happened to you if Larry here hadn't intervened. He saved you from a terrible experience, he saved you from an awful death. I want you to apologize to Mr. Adams for calling him a bastard, after you give him his money. Now, Jill."

Jill stubbornly walked up the hill, heading for the beach. Half way up, she stopped and yelled back.

"OK, so you aren't a bastard. Thanks."

As she continued up the hill a troubled look crossed her face. She peeked back at the dead body of Raoul laying in the dusty street. A shudder shook her small body and a few wayward tears fought their way out of her eyes. And then suddenly she had no strength left and she sat down on a rock, put her broken face in her hands, and cried and cried and cried as she tried to cover her tortured chest with what little clothes she had left. Remembering again the rapist's fingers tearing at her, remembering Raoul's cigarette burning her.

A half of an hour later, she stood in front of her pirate with a face recently washed in salt water and handed him her backpack. She stood as tall and as proud as she could.

"Thank you, Mr. Adams, for saving my family and myself. I hope we weren't an inconvenience to you. All of your money is there except a little bit I took out for wear and tear of the boat." Her father gave her a fierce glare. "But on second thought," she pulled a wad out of her pocket, here is the rest. Thank you, kind sir, for killing the bad guys. Sorry I ever called you, 'bastard'. I apologize for it. I hope you will remember your time with us in a happy light."

Janet was smiling from ear to ear as she looked on Jill with pride. Her little girl was really growing up.

"Damn rotten kid. But you got spunk. Here." He forced the wad of expense money back at her. She grabbed it, stepped back, and forced it into her pockets before he could change his mind. He reached out to her. He held the back of her neck with one hand and gently pulled her nose with the other. With a snap her broken nose was realigned and she could breath again.

"Janet, get some water and clean up the girl. Harv. Come here, let's look at that hand." He took Harv's hand into his own and gently felt the surface. He let the hand tell him what was wrong. He felt for the heat and vibration of fiercely flowing blood. An intent look crossed his face and suddenly sweat beads popped out all over his face. He closed his eyes with the effort.

Harv felt as if someone was controlling his hand. The fingers started to move, all by themselves. His hand suddenly made a fist and then opened again. Then it lay quiet between Larry's hands.

"That's all I can do for you. You have to use the hand. Work with it, use it. If you baby it, it will wither up and die. It'll hurt. It'll hurt one hell of a lot. But life hurts, man, life hurts. Get used to it. Live with it. Embrace it. Fuck, its only pain."

With that he opened the car door and started the motor. He looked over at Janney. Close to her, he recognized her as that chick on the motor boat he couldn't start.

"You going to get any blood on my upholstery?" She shook her head no. Janet helped her into the passenger side. Then she walked around to the driver side and slid her head in through the window. Swiftly, before she lost her nerve she kissed Larry full on the lips. Again her body started to react to him. She didn't fight it. She took his spirit into her through her lips, it seemed to come out of him, almost like smoke. Then quickly she pulled her head out of the car.

"Thanks, for Harv's hand, thanks for saving Jill, thanks for caring for us here. You are a good man, Larry or Volcano, or whatever your name is. You might be a crook, a pirate, a killer, a rapist, but you are a good man. Your secrets are safe with us. We won't tell. And I'll, I'll never forget you."

Larry put the car into gear and backed it up away from the tree. He looked out at Harv, Janet and Jill, all staring at him.

"Work the hand," he told Harv.

"If it is about the survival of the fittest, then become the fittest," he told Jill.

"Love is a power that can work miracles. Everyone has the power, but few have the will to use it. Practice," he told Janet.

He stepped on the gas and the car was gone in a cloud of dust.

XLVIII

Cabo San Lucas, Baja

Harv walked down the beautiful crystal sand beach of Cabo San Lucas carrying two beers in the fingers of his right hand and a coke in his left. Janet and Jill were sun bathing on the beach and smiling at the Mexican vendors as they wandered by offering everything under the sun. For some reason Janet had just bought a huge ceramic pig which was stuck in the sand next to their towels. The pig only encouraged the other salesmen.

"Here you go girls, get something cold inside of you," he smiled at them. "And what is that?" he groaned, pointing at the pig.

"It is my mascot, Honey. You know you said I couldn't have a dog as the boat was too small, well, so I got a pig!" Harv stared at it lost for words.

"Where is it going to live? There isn't a locker on the boat big enough for it. It is big enough to take up a whole berth. No. Sorry. It can't be allowed. You will have to take it back."

"Honey, I can't. The man that sold it to me ran off saying something about today being his lucky day. I think he was going to get a lotto ticket. Anyway, I like it. I think it is cute."

"If you two are finished arguing, someone is trying to get a suntan. If I get lines in my tan, I will know who, whom to blame. But thanks for the coke, Dad. I think the pig is atrocious too. I think the guy who sold it was tired of carrying it around. I mean, for 2 bucks? How could Mom turn down anything for 2 bucks?"

Suddenly Harv started to laugh. It was all so normal. So touristy. So different from their trip down the coast. They were no different than any of the other hundreds of people on the beach.

"Yes, we are," he mumbled, "we are the only ones with our own giant pig mascot!"

"What was that, honey?"

"We can use your pig as an attack dog. No one would dare come on the boat with such a monstrosity guarding the deck!"

Janet started to look offended but the suddenly started to laugh, and laugh, and laugh. Harv grabbed her hand and pulled her into the clear, warm water with a big splash. Jill wasn't far behind and the three of them couldn't stop laughing and hugging each other for the rest of the day.

XLIX

City of San Diego

Larry looked out of the dusty windscreen. Janney had tried to clean it for him. He had stopped her with a hand on her arm.

"If we can't see out, then anyone outside, definitely can't see in. I like it that way."

They were waiting across the street from the city jail. Larry had found out on the internet that Lucy had been tried, found guilty and had been sentenced to life in prison with no parole. She was scheduled to be transferred to a long term facility for lifers. There would be no educational possibilities there, no library, no TV, nothing to remind the inmates of the world outside. No, nothing at all, except for a chaplain.

Larry hadn't been able to determine which facility she was being moved to. So here he was waiting. He wasn't sure why. The last place in the world he should be is in this town. This San Diego. His mug shot would still be in every cop's mind. They would still be hoping for a big collar, and the hope for promotion.

"Fuck, what the hell am I doing here, damn it," he swore to himself under his breath. "I am so going to get out of this pig pen of a city. It was safer down in Mexico." It was too late to leave now. There were cops all over the street and the parking lot as the inmates were lead out. Their ankles were cuffed six inches apart so they shuffled along as they came out. Their hands were cuffed behind their backs and then tied to a chain around their waists which led to the cuffs on their feet. They were making sure there were going to be no jail breaks on this trip.

He saw her then. He thought it was her. She looked different somehow. She didn't stand as straight as she used to. She used to stand so tall, so proud, so sure of herself, so sure that the world loved her. Now, now it was if she was a used, discarded condom. A thing of no worth. A thing fit only for the garbage can.

For a minute, Larry thought it wasn't her. It couldn't be. It must be someone who just looked like her. But, no. It was her. She had done some hard time. Very hard time.

"Fuck it.   She   was   worth   twenty   pimply   assistant managers." His eyes narrowed as he watched the pigs force her into the pig wagon. One of them slapped her across the rump. He laughed about it with the other screws. She didn't even react.

"It shouldn't be allowed.   Fuck it to hell."   His eyes narrowed into slits. His lips compressed. He turned both eyes, full faced, at the police van and stared hard at the screws. Then he gave a little smile.

The van pulled out into traffic and Larry followed it staying five cars back.   Soon it became apparent that they were heading north to LA. Larry sped ahead and just before the freeway's onramp, he pulled over, got out of the car and walked out into the first traffic lane.   He stared at the approaching police transport van, traveling at 65 MPH with a mild expression on his face. Janney switched over to the driver side and pulled the car up a quarter of a mile down the road.

She didn't know exactly what he was going to do. She knew she was to drive the car and to be ready to pick him up when he signaled. He said his plans might change at any time so she had to be alert. He would wave his hand when he wanted to be picked up.

Janney thought about just driving off when he waved his hand. About driving off and giving him the finger. For what he had done to her. The only thing was he had done all those things again during the last two weeks. Done them every night. Done them in the middle of the day. She had gotten to the point where she actually liked it. Where she wanted it. Where she needed it. She had gotten to the point where she got crabby if he hadn't screwed her in the last eight hours. She had started thinking she might actually like the bastard. Like him enough to stay with him till she could screw him out of all his money. The bastard.

L

San Diego

"Hey," said Ton. "There's a guy standing in the road. Guy's gotta be on crack or something." His real name was Tom, but since he weighed well over 250 pounds, all of it muscle, and was short, everyone called him One Ton, or just Ton. He didn't mind. He was easy going. He did what he was told. If they told him to rough up a prisoner, he didn't mind. Wasn't anything to do with him. He was just obeying orders.

"Christ, yeah," shouted Spud. "Hey, 3 points if you can run him down, Ton!" Spud also weighed over 250 pounds, but all of it was fat. He was the fattest man in the prison. It wasn't his fault. They had good food at the prison. For the guards, anyway. The cons? They got anything left after the guards had their fill and spit in the rest. Spud, he liked to beat up people while others held them down. It made him feel like a man. God knows, no woman would ever let him touch them.

"Make it 10 points, and you're on!" yelled Ton with a

whoop. His eyes lit up and he gripped the steering wheel harder.

"Ton, slow down. You hit him and we will be sitting around filling out paper work for 2 days," said the Captain. He wasn't a Captain. He was a screw like the rest of them, but he liked to give orders, and he liked to be called 'The Captain.'

"You ain't no god damn Captain. Who says Ton can't hit him and drive on, huh? Huh, wise guy? Who the fuck died and made you god, anyway. Hit him, Ton. I give you twenty, you hit him."

"Ton, you even come close, you is fired, suspended, and I lock you up myself."

"Hey, guys," Ton broke in, "Look, he is that perp, that Volcano, who was with that blond broad in back in that store where's they killed the manager and cut off his fingers. See' em? It's him. I swear, it's him."

"God, yeah, you right, Ton. God Damn, Yeah. Hit him, Ton. We is doing our civic duty killing off criminals like'n him. Get him, Ton! I give you thirty just to see you do it!"

"Ton, slow down, stop in front of him. That is a collar, boys. That is a collar and a promotion. Downtown, they been looking for this guy, like forever. We get him, and damn, we get our pictures in the paper. Like as not, we get a raise, too. Looks like he wants ta give his self up, too. Look at 'em, just standing there."

The van stopped a couple of feet from Larry. He never moved. Not even an inch. The Captain and Spud have fell out of the cab in their excitement.

"Hey, you, perp. Get you fucking hands behind your head," commanded Spud. The Captain pulled out his service revolver, cocked it, and aimed it at Larry's head.

Larry mildly put his hands behind his head. He looked down at the ground and never said a word.

"Ton," yelled The Captain excitedly, "Bring some cuffs, lots of 'em. Hurry up, now."

Ton came down and started to cuff Larry behind his back. As soon as he had his wrists and ankles secured, Spud hauled off and hit Larry right in the solar plexus with everything he had. Then he roughly searched him.

"Asshole ain't got no gun or no knife. The fuck, why was this guy standing out here, anyway?"

"Don't matter, Spud," sneered The Captain. "He is ours now. We is going a be rich, boys!"

"Yeah, how you like those apples, Volcano, or what ever the fuck you is calling yourself these days," cursed Spud and slapped him across the head with an open palm so as to not leave any marks.

They grabbed his arms and frog marched him to the rear of the van and roughly shoved him in.

"Hey," said Ton, "do you think we should of read him his rights? They do that in all the cop shows."

"Fuckers like that ain't got no fucking rights. And ain't that the fucking truth?" Cursed Spud. The other two nodded.

"Yeah, fucker don't have no goddamn rights," echoed Ton.

LI

Freeways of San Diego

It was dark inside the van. A little light came in through two slit windows high up the side. Larry rolled over to a sitting position and worked a pack of matches out of his pocket. He tore one out and shoved it down the tooth side of the ratchet of one of the cuffs. He worked gently and he heard a click as the match end depressed the spring loaded bar into its casing. Holding the match in place he carefully pulled out the swinging part of the bracelet. It took several goes to get it released. With one hand free, it was only seconds till he had his feet and other hand free. The cops had clamped the cuffs on his wrists as tight as they could, so he had kept his fingers straight as it takes more muscles to extend a hand than it does to make a fist. Fingers extended, his wrist was much larger.

He looked around and located Lucy. She was sitting in a corner and staring at the floor. She hadn't even looked up when they threw Larry into the van. He touched her hair. Suddenly he was reassured. It was Lucy. She was still in there some where. Hidden away, sure, but all of her was not destroyed. In a matter of seconds, he had her un-cuffed. He threw the matches to the other cons who had been watching the proceedings with open, staring, interested eyes. He helped

Lucy over to the door and pulled two short shivs out from the soles of his shoes.

Carefully he inserted them between the door and the van, one above and one below the lock. Gently he pushed down on the dead bolt with first one shiv and then the other. Push down, twist the dead bolt into the door, do it with the other. Time after time. He almost had it made when the van went over a bump in the road and he had to start all over. He was faster this time. Finally he had the door open. He held it, just ajar, till he felt the van slowing for an off ramp. He threw open the door, grabbed Lucy in his arms, and jumped.

He lost his footing after ten feet and the two of them rolled down the road for a bit. Larry found his feet, pulled Lucy up, just as Janney pulled up in the car. Larry shoved Lucy in the back seat, jumped into the driver's seat, did a u turn and was off. In his rear view mirror he saw cons jumping out of the van and running every which way.

'Mexico, here I come,' he thought to himself.

It was no trouble crossing the border. He left the stolen car at a shopping mall and they walked across, as if they were visiting Tijuana just for the day. No one stopped them. No one even looked at them. Across the way, where the traffic and people on foot were returning to America the line stretched for miles. But not for going into Mexico. In Tijuana, he stole a car with California plates, headed south and east and was soon zipping along desert roads in the wilds of Poncho Villa's old haunts.

LII

Somewhere in Mexico

Janney stayed with them. She knew she was a third wheel. She didn't care. The sex was so good. She had always been a sexual creature deep inside, but she had always kept that aspect of her personality hidden since childhood. Now, with Volcano, it didn't matter. He didn't ask first if she would like to try something. He just did it. And he did it so well. He seemed to turn her on so easily. She had forgotten about getting even with Volcano. She called him Larry now. Sometimes she thought she was in love with him. Janney didn't know if the sex was so good because of who he was or despite of it. And she didn't care. She really didn't. Just keep it coming, for as long as it lasted, that's what she wanted. She didn't even mind that some days she could hardly walk, what with all the spasms radiating out of her belly for hours and hours after they had finished. Her legs felt so weak afterwards. She didn't care if her brain seemed to turn off sometimes. Thinking was over rated anyway. Her body's demands came first. She was just happy she got the lion's share of the sex while Lucy was recovering. Then one day, at dawn, Lucy woke up and started laughing.

"Larry! Hey, Larry? You wouldn't believe the dream I just had! God, it was awful. It seemed so real. But it was just a dream, wasn't it Larry?"

"Just a dream, doll, just a dream."

They had wandered down to the Mexican Rivera. Larry's money went a long ways down there and no one looked twice at one guy shacked up with two beautiful women. As Lucy regained her strength and sanity, Larry started planning.

"Well, ladies. What do you say we go back to work? I know this nice little bull ring just down the road, that doesn't bank till Monday morning.

"You girls want to have some fun?"

And he smiled his little smile.